Praise for the 'Alice & Megan' series

'Brilliantly observed', *Evening Echo*

'Girls and boys will warm to Judi Curtin's funny

stories about friendship', *The Sunday Independent*

JUDI CURTIN grew up in Cork and now lives in Limerick where she is married with three children. Judi is the best-selling author of the 'Alice & Megan' series and the 'Eva' series; with Roisin Meaney, she is also the author of *See If I Care,* and she has written three novels, *Sorry, Walter, From Claire to Here* and *Almost Perfect.* Her books have been translated into many languages.

The 'Alice & Megan' series
Alice Next Door

Alice Again

Don't Ask Alice

Alice in the Middle

Bonjour Alice

Alice & Megan Forever

Alice to the Rescue

Alice & Megan's Cookbook

The 'Eva' series
Eva's Journey

Eva's Holiday

Leave it to Eva

Eva and the Hidden Diary

VIVA ALICE!

THE O'BRIEN PRESS
DUBLIN

First published 2014 by
The O'Brien Press Ltd,
12 Terenure Road East,
Rathgar, Dublin 6,
Ireland.
Tel: +353 1 4923333
Fax: +353 1 4922777
E-mail: books@obrien.ie
Website: www.obrien.ie

ISBN: 978-1-84717-665-3

8 7 6 5 4 3 2 1
18 17 16 15 14

Printed and bound by CPI Group (UK) Ltd, Croydon, CR0 4YY
The paper in this book is produced using pulp from managed forests

The O'Brien Press receives financial assistance from

DEDICATION

For Dan, Brian, Ellen and Annie.

ACKNOWLEDGEMENTS

Big thanks to everyone at The O'Brien Press for their continuing support and enthusiasm. Extra-big thanks to super-editor Helen Carr – once again, you've been great.

Chapter One

'**O**migod, Megan. You've got to come over to my place right now,' said Alice, racing into the kitchen and grabbing my arm. 'It's an emergency.'

Mum looked up from the bundle of broccoli she was washing.

'I don't care if it's an emergency, Megan,' she said. 'You're not going anywhere until you finish your porridge.'

Mum has known my best friend for thirteen years. I guess she understands that Alice has drama queen moments. I shovelled the last few spoons of porridge into my mouth, and got up from the table.

'Dishwasher,' said Mum, without even looking up.

I sighed and put my bowl into the dishwasher. My cat, who was curled up in the corner of the kitchen, looked up at me mournfully.

'Sorry, Domino,' I said. 'No time for cuddles. Didn't you hear? This is an emergency.'

Domino put on her best sulky-cat face and went back to cleaning her paws as I followed Alice outside.

'What is it?' I asked. 'What's going on?'

'It's my mum. She's gone crazy.'

I raised one eyebrow and Alice giggled. 'OK, so she's gone even crazier than usual.'

Alice's mum and my mum are both crazy in their own, very different, ways. My mum is obsessed with saving the world, and feeding my sister Rosie and me with tons of organic fruit and vegetables. Alice's mum is obsessed with how she looks, and spends most of her time visiting hair and nail salons.

'What's she done *this* time?' I asked.

'She's planning a party for Jamie's birthday.'

'What's crazy about that?'

'She's invited half the kids in his class, and ...'

'And what?'

'And she wants to have the party in our apartment.'

Alice's voice was all weird when she said the last words, and I couldn't decide if she was trying not to laugh, or trying not to cry. Maybe it was a bit of both.

'You've got to be kidding,' I said.

'Nope. Like I said, my mum's finally slipped over the edge. She's officially gone crazy.'

I thought about arguing with her, but I couldn't do it. It *did* sound like Alice's mum had lost it. For most mums, having a party in your own apartment wouldn't be a big deal. Alice's mum isn't like most mums, though. Her apartment is all white and shiny and perfect. Things like a crumb on the floor or a greasy handprint on a wall are like major disasters as far as she is concerned.

When Alice was little, she was never allowed to have her parties at home – they always had to be in cinemas or restaurants or activity centres.

'But I don't understand,' I said. 'Doesn't your mum know that Jamie's friends will trash the apartment? That's going to drive her crazy.'

'I tried telling her, but she won't listen to me. Ever since I fell out of the tree and ended up in hospital, Mum's been acting really weird. She says she feels guilty about what happened, and that she should have been a better mother to Jamie and me. She says that from now on, she's going to be a "hands-on" mum. It's going to end in tears, I just know it.'

Once again, I couldn't argue. Trying to be a better person is probably a good thing, but didn't Veronica understand that it couldn't happen overnight? There's no such thing as an instant personality transplant – if there was, I'd book my mum in for one.

'OK, Alice,' I said. 'For once, I have to agree with you. I think this might well be an emergency. We'd better go over to your place and see how bad things are.'

★ ★ ★

Alice's mum, Veronica, was sitting at the kitchen table. Her hair was all messy and her usually perfect nails were all chipped and broken, like she'd been chewing them.

She was flipping madly through a pile of pages she'd printed from the computer.

'Second best won't do,' she muttered. 'This party just *has* to be perfect.'

'Do something, Megan,' whispered Alice. 'Please.'

I've always been a bit afraid of Veronica, but I knew I had to be brave.

'Er, Veronica,' I said. 'Maybe you need to rethink this whole party thing. Boys of Jamie's age can be a bit wild sometimes. Maybe it would be better if you—'

Veronica looked up at me with a scary look in her eyes. 'It's a bit too late for rethinking,' she said. 'I hand-delivered the invitations last night. No matter what happens, the party is going ahead tomorrow.'

I gulped. 'Tomorrow? Are you sure that's a good idea?'

Veronica gave a crazy laugh. 'Why ever not? Your mother always has lovely parties for you and Rosie. How hard can it be?'

Very hard?

My mum always starts planning our parties weeks in advance.

And she likes being around small kids.

And she likes cooking.

And she doesn't care if our house gets trashed.

I was wondering how to answer Veronica, when I realised it didn't matter what I said. Veronica had already forgotten about me. She'd gone back to studying her printouts, and she was adding notes to a very long list.

I knew it was time for damage limitation.

'Maybe Alice and I could help you,' I said. 'I could even ask my mum to come over for a bit. She actually likes organising parties and she's quite good at it. I know she'd be glad to—'

'No,' said Veronica in a high-pitched voice, like I'd just offered to stab her or something. 'No need to involve your mother in this. Thank you anyway, Megan, but everything is under control. Leave it to me – Jamie is going to have a party he will *never* forget.'

Chapter Two

The next day, Mum wouldn't let me go out until I'd done my history project on medieval castles. It took ages and ages and every time I thought it was finished, Mum thought of something else I should include.

'I've got a great idea,' she said, when I finally closed up my folder. 'When you're making your presentation, why don't you dress up as a girl from medieval times? I've got some lovely material you could use to make a dress. You just wait here while I go and ......'

Before she'd finished her sentence, she jumped up and ran out of the room. By the time I caught up with her, she was halfway up the ladder into the attic.

'Mum!' I wailed. 'I'm not in primary school

any more. If I dress up, everyone will just laugh at me.'

She came back down the ladder. 'I was only trying to help,' she said.

'I know,' I said. 'And I'm grateful, really I am. But trust me, my project is finished. I need to go to Alice's place now, OK?'

'We could make you a medieval headdress,' she said. 'That wouldn't take long, and you'd look absolutely beautiful with a—'

'Mum!' I said. 'Do you want me to look like a total loser?'

She stopped arguing then. She doesn't really know what a loser is, but I guess she knows it's not a good thing.

'Thanks for your help,' I said again. 'Now I really, really need to go. Alice needs me.'

Mum hugged me, and finally I was free to leave.

★　★　★

Alice's face was white when she met me at the door.

'Don't say anything,' she said, as she led me inside.

Veronica's normally perfect apartment was a total mess. Limp balloons and tangled streamers hung from every corner. A big banner hung over the living room door. I read the words aloud – '*HAPPY BIRTHDAY JAM*'. Alice gave a hysterical giggle. 'The printer ran out of ink before it was finished,' she said. 'I thought about going to the shop to get more ink, but in the end I didn't dare. I was afraid to leave Mum on her own.'

I turned to look at the dining area. Every single surface was covered with dishes of weird-looking food.

'It's a total disaster,' whispered Alice. 'Nothing went right. The popcorn didn't pop, the jelly didn't set, the cupcakes sank and the birthday cake … it's meant to be an aeroplane but …'

She pointed at the birthday cake and didn't

say any more. She didn't need to.

If you looked *very* carefully, you could see that it was meant to be a plane – but it looked like one that had crash-landed from a long way up. A wing and a wheel had fallen off, and the front was all smashed up. Chocolate icing dripped down one side, and was spreading slowly across the table like lumpy brown lava. It was like something out of a very bad horror movie – the kind my mum doesn't let me watch.

In the corner of the room, Alice's brother, Jamie, was curled up on a chair, flicking through the pages of a book about wizards. Usually he's a bit wild, but now he just looked sad and miserable. I felt sorry for him.

'He's only little,' whispered Alice. 'But even he knows that this is shaping up to be the worst party in the history of the world. You've got to help us, Megan. You've just got to.'

Before I could answer, the doorbell rang and Veronica appeared from the bedroom. She looked wild and crazy.

'They're here!' she said in the high-pitched voice that scared me so much. 'The guests are here.'

Then she tottered towards the door, almost falling on her super-high heels.

I thought about going to hide under Alice's bed until the whole thing was over, but I knew I couldn't do that. My friend needed me – so it was a pity that I had *no* idea how I was going to help her.

Chapter Three

Ten minutes later, seventeen small kids were gathered in the living room. Nobody was saying anything as everyone looked at the sad display of food.

In the end a little girl with curly blonde hair spoke. 'What kind of a stupid party is this?' she asked in a spoiled voice. 'The food is all messy and I don't like it.'

The boy next to her poked his dirty finger into a bowl of runny green jelly that looked a bit like frogspawn. 'This is loser food,' he said. 'And I want to go home.'

In a corner of the room, Alice and Veronica stood as if they'd been turned to stone. It was like they'd gone ahead and started their own private game of statues, without inviting anyone else to join in.

I looked at Jamie. He was standing on his own at the end of the table. His bottom lip was wobbling and his eyes were filling up with tears. He can be a total pain sometimes, but the poor little boy didn't deserve this. I figured I had about fifteen seconds to come up with a plan.

'Hey, kids,' I said suddenly. 'Guess what?'

'What?' asked a small freckly boy.

I hadn't thought of an answer yet, so I played for time.

'Come closer,' I said. 'Huddle up near me and I'll tell you a big, huge secret.'

The kids obediently came close and stood in a small circle in front of me. Seventeen pairs of eyes gazed up at me, as if I had something important to say. I really, really wished I had something important to say

'Er ... you'll never guess what?' I said again.

'What?' asked the freckly boy again.

'Er ... well ... this morning ... something totally amazing happened here.'

'What was it?' asked the blonde girl.

'Well ... you see ... during the night ... Jamie's mum cooked all this super-special party food. It was so beautiful, people were going to come from a magazine to take pictures of it. It was going to be on a tv show, all about amazing parties.'

'But the food *isn't* amazing,' said the freckly boy. 'It's all messy and horrible. It looks like a big stinky giant puked it up.'

When he said this, some of the kids laughed, and the others screamed and made faces. I was thinking about giving up, when I looked at Jamie again. He was staring at me, like I was the only one in the world who could save his party. (The scary thing is, he was probably right.)

I took a deep breath and went on with my

story. 'The food is messy because, before the tv and magazine people got here, something terrible happened.'

'What?' asked a little girl with huge blue eyes. 'Hurry up and tell us.'

I wouldn't have minded hurrying up. The only problem was, I had no idea what I was going to say next. Veronica and Alice were staring at me, like I knew what I was doing. I looked frantically around the room, and spotted the wizard book that Jamie had been reading earlier.

'A wicked wizard came here,' I said quickly. 'Right into this very room. His broomstick was broken and he wanted to steal the aeroplane cake to fly home on.'

'How did he get in?' asked a boy.

'Through the door,' I said. 'Jamie's mum left it open by mistake.'

'That cake isn't big enough for a wizard to fly on,' he said.

'It was a small wizard,' I said. 'Now, stop

interrupting and let me get on with the story. The brave cake didn't want to help the wicked wizard, so it deliberately crash-landed on the table and the wizard fell off and bumped his head on the floor.'

'Yay!' yelled all the kids together.

'I can see the mark on the floor where the wizard bumped his head,' said the freckly boy. 'Amn't I clever?'

I ignored him. 'And the wizard was *so* angry,' I said. 'He cast a spell on the beautiful food, and made it look all messy. Then he ran back out the door before anyone saw him.'

'If no one saw him, how do *you* know it happened?' asked the boy.

'Because I know everything,' I said, glaring at him.

'I'm scared of wizards,' said the girl with the big blue eyes. 'Is he going to come back?'

I smiled at her. 'No, I don't think so. Not if that silly boy stops asking silly questions. Now let's play some games and after that we can eat all the delicious, magically-messy food. How does that sound?'

'Yay!' shouted all the kids together again.

Alice came over and hugged me. 'You're a genius, Megan,' she said. 'A total genius.'

★　★　★

Alice helped me to organise lots of games. We played dead wizards and flying wizards and lost wizards and statue wizards. The kids were having a great time, and after a bit, Veronica recovered enough to want to join in.

'Let's have a competition to see who can make up the best spell,' she said. 'Who wants to go first?'

No one said anything, and Veronica started to look nervous.

'Whoever goes first can have a sweet,' she said.

'*One* sweet?' said a boy. 'Is that all?'

'All right then, a whole packet of sweets,'

said Veronica.

'OK, I'll start,' the boy said, grinning. 'It's a spell to turn girls into gross, slimy maggots.'

All the girls started screaming and pretending to vomit, and all the boys laughed like it was the funniest thing they'd ever heard in their lives.

Then the boy continued. 'All you need is a big bowl of cat's wee-wee, and you mix that with a bowl of dog's vomit, and then you get a stinky dirty nappy—'

Now Veronica shrieked too. 'That's enough, you silly little boy. We don't want to hear that kind of thing do we, children?'

'Yes, we do,' shouted another boy.

'He's making me feel sick,' said a small girl. 'I don't like talking about rude things.'

'I want my sweets,' said the first boy. 'You promised me. If I don't get my sweets I'm going to—'

I could see that things were getting out of hand.

'Maybe it's time for food?' I said to Veronica.
She nodded and ran to get matches to light
the candles on the cake. I crossed my fingers,
hoping she wasn't going to burn the house
down. After all my trouble, that would have
been kind of a disappointing end to the party.

★　★　★

An hour later, all the kids had gone home, and
Alice and I had helped Veronica to tidy up.
Except for a few small chocolate stains on the
carpet, the place looked pretty ok.

Veronica hugged me.

'Thanks, Megan,' she said. 'I think you might
have saved all of our lives.'

I blushed, but I didn't argue. I think she
might have been right.

Chapter Four

'Three more days till the Easter holidays,' said Alice as she walked me home. 'It'll be nice to be off school, but I wish we were going somewhere nice. I wish we were ...'

She stopped talking – probably because I'd grabbed her arm and was squeezing it tightly.

'Hey, that hurts,' she said. 'Why are you ...?'

Instead of answering, I used my free hand to point along the road.

'Oh,' said Alice. 'Now I get it.'

The meanest girl in the world was walking

towards us. I walked slower and slower, but even so, we were soon face to face with her.

'Hi, Megan. Hi Alice,' she said.

'Hi, Melissa,' we both replied.

I've known Melissa since we were in primary school together, and I've always been a bit afraid of her. When we all started secondary school, and she decided to go away to boarding school, I felt like she'd given me a huge present. She comes home most weekends, though, and I always seem to bump in to her. Sometimes I think it's like she's stalking me or something.

Once Melissa had a moment of weakness and told me that she hated boarding school, but mostly she just brags about the fancy swimming pool and the fancy riding stables and the fancy chefs who cook fancy food for the students. When she gets tired of bragging, she usually starts to pick on me. She always gives me a hard time about my mum's weird environmental ideas. Last time we met, she'd mocked me because I was wearing the scarf

Mum had knitted for my thirteenth birthday. (I admit the scarf is fairly gross, but that's not really the point.)

'So what's happening around here these days?' asked Melissa now. 'All boring stuff, I suppose.'

'I'm just walking Megan home after Jamie's birthday party,' said Alice.

'Oh,' said Melissa with a big fake smile. 'Poor Megan, I guess you never get asked to proper parties so you just go to little kids ones.'

'Megan was helping to organise the party,' said Alice. 'And she was really good.'

Alice was trying to help me, but I knew she was wasting her time.

'How nice,' said Melissa in a sick, sweet voice. 'Let me guess, Megan. Did you knit a birthday cake and crochet a pizza and make a jug of yummy nettle juice to wash it all down?'

I wanted to say something smart back, but when Melissa's around, it's like my brain goes into slow motion. I opened my mouth and no words came out. As usual, Alice came to my rescue.

'That doesn't even make sense, Melissa,' she said. 'I know you're always kind of dumb, but I see you're making a special effort today. We're honoured, aren't we, Megan?'

I giggled.

'Totally,' I said.

Melissa's mouth went all wrinkly, like she'd just sucked a super-sour lemon. She loves saying mean stuff to me, but she doesn't much like it when people do the same to her.

'You're *so* immature, you two,' she said, and then she tossed her golden curls and marched off, with the heels of her fancy boots making loud clicky-clacky sounds on the footpath.

'Thanks for that, Al,' I said.

She smiled at me. 'No worries. As long as I'm around, Melissa will never get away with being mean to you.'

'Thanks,' I said again.

She was being nice, but her words scared me

a bit. Alice isn't super-glued to my side, and I wondered if I'd ever be brave enough to stand up to Melissa on my own.

★ ★ ★

An hour later, I was lying on my bed reading when the doorbell rang. From the hall, I could hear my friend, Grace, fighting off Mum's efforts to give her a glass of carrot juice and a sugar-free cookie. Then I heard her explaining to my little sister Rosie why she couldn't go into her bedroom and play dressing-up. Finally she arrived in my room.

'Hey, Megan, I've got brilliant news,' she said. 'Mum and Dad have decided to book a last-minute Easter trip to our villa in Lanzarote.'

'That's so cool,' I said. 'You're really lucky. Alice and I were saying how nice it would be to go away for the holidays.'

'I haven't told you the best news yet,' said Grace. 'Mum and Dad said I can bring two friends ... and ...'

She stopped talking while she took off her jacket and threw herself onto the end of my bed.

I hardly dared to hope. Grace has heaps of friends, so what were the chances of her choosing me?

'... and,' she continued when she was comfortable. 'Louise is going to stay with her cousins for Easter and Kellie is going to pony camp, so even if I asked them, they wouldn't be able to come.'

I let myself feel the tiniest bit excited.

'And I called over to Alice's place a few minutes ago,' she continued. 'And she's allowed to come and I was kind of wondering if ...'

I sat up straight.

Was Grace going to say what I hoped she was going to say?

Was this going to turn into the best Easter holidays ever?

Grace was lying there, twiddling her hair,

like what she had to say wasn't really all that important. I felt like shaking her, but decided that wasn't a good plan. Finally she finished her sentence. '... if you'd like to come too?'

'OMG,' I squealed, as I threw myself on top of her. 'I'd *so* love to come. It would be totally amazing. It would be the best thing ever. It would be ...'

I stopped and stood up slowly. It was never going to happen. Flights to Lanzarote were bound to be expensive, and Mum was saving up for a new greenhouse.

'There's a half-price flight sale on at the moment,' said Grace, like she could read my mind.

My hopes rose again before she ruined things with her next words. 'The sale ends at midnight tonight.'

My mum would never make up her mind that quickly. First she'd have to contact the FBI to make sure no one in Grace's family had ever, ever done anything wrong. Then she'd have to do a big research project on the quality of the organic vegetables in Lanzarote. Then she'd have to worry about crime and sunburn and food poisoning and insect bites. It was hopeless.

Once again Grace read my mind. 'Why don't you ask your mum and dad now?'

'Yeah, why not?' I said.

Might as well get it over with, so when they say no, Grace can go ahead and ask someone else.

Grace followed me into the kitchen where Mum and Dad were sitting at the table drinking some gross-smelling herbal tea.

'Grace has invited me to go to Lanzarote with her family next week,' I said quickly. 'Can I go? Please? Please? There's a flight sale, so it won't even be expensive, and I've saved some of my Confirmation money, so I could pay half if you want. Please Mum and Dad, please can I go?'

As usual, Dad didn't answer. He just looked at Mum and waited to see what she had to say.

As usual, that was a lot.

'That's very kind of you and your family, Grace,' she said. 'But Donal and I have a lot to think about before we say yes or no. It's all a bit of a rush, and I'm not sure we'll have time to make an informed decision.'

I put my head down. I should have known I was wasting my time. The holiday would be over, and Grace and Alice's suntans would be faded by the time my mum finished her investigations.

'It doesn't matter,' I said. 'I know it's not going to happen. I shouldn't even have asked.'

Mum didn't say anything else. She stared at me and I couldn't figure out what she was thinking.

'Come on, Grace,' I said. 'Let's go.'

Grace followed me back to my room. 'Your mum didn't actually say no,' she said. 'Maybe you should give her a chance to think about it.'

I shook my head. 'You don't know her like I do. I'm sorry, Grace, but maybe you'd better start thinking about who else you could ask to go to Lanzarote with you. What about one of the girls from your class? Or maybe ...'

Tears came to my eyes and I couldn't finish. Why did I have to be stuck with the weirdest, fussiest mum in the history of the universe?

It just wasn't fair.

Chapter Five

A few minutes later the doorbell rang again. I didn't know what to say when I saw Veronica and Alice standing on the door-step. Alice was grinning like a crazy person. Veronica was all neat and tidy and back to her old, scary self.

'Hello, Megan,' said Veronica. 'I wonder if I could speak to your parents for a moment?'

I knew I hadn't done anything wrong, but still I felt nervous.

Why was Veronica here?

What was she going to say?

'Er … I guess so,' I said. 'Come on in.'

Veronica followed me towards the kitchen. Grace appeared from my room, and she stood in the hall with Alice, whispering and giggling. I guessed they were talking about all the cool things they were going to do in Lanzarote.

Suddenly I felt jealous.

Was my Easter going to be totally ruined?

Were my two friends going to go to Lanzarote and have an amazing time, while I was stuck at home doing boring stuff, as usual?

'Veronica!' said Mum. She jumped up from the table, as she tried to fix her wild hair. 'So nice to see you. Would you like a cup of yarrow tea?'

'Thank you, Sheila, but no,' said Veronica. 'This is just a quick visit. I came to tell you and Donal what a great help Megan was this afternoon. She organised Jamie's party and thanks to her it turned out to be a huge success. She's a great girl, and an absolute credit to you both.'

'Well, I—' began Mum, but Veronica didn't let her finish. Maybe the fact that Mum was walking towards the kettle, and waving a yarrow tea-bag in the air, was making her nervous.

'Anyway, that was all I had to say,' said Veronica quickly, as she went back into the hall. 'Thanks again for your help, Megan. Come along, Alice.'

Alice winked madly at me and grabbed Grace's arm. 'Megan has a lot to discuss with her mum and dad,' she said. 'Why don't we wait for her outside?'

I watched as Mum closed the front door behind Veronica, Grace and Alice.

What on earth was that all about?

Mum came back into the kitchen and hugged me. 'Well done, Megan,' she said. 'It was nice of you to help Veronica. That poor woman can hardly control her own little boy, much less a whole room full of lively children. I dread to think what would have happened if you hadn't been there. Someone might have been killed.'

She was exaggerating a bit, but I didn't care – because I suddenly understood what was going on.

'Er, Mum, about Lanzarote? You never

exactly gave me a final answer.'

Mum looked at Dad, and he looked at her, and I looked at them both, and suddenly a miracle happened.

Mum smiled. 'I'm very impressed with what Veronica had to say about you, Megan,' she said. 'You've been unusually mature and sensible lately, and maybe we should let you go away with Grace and her family. What do you think, Donal?'

Dad smiled too, and I started to feel all breathless and excited.

'So I can go?' I asked. 'I can really go?'

Mum didn't answer, and I knew that was a good result.

I raced over and hugged them both, and Mum nearly spilled her yarrow tea, and Dad dropped his sugar-free cookie, and Domino raced over and ate it, and Rosie came running in to see what all the fuss was about.

And I thought I was going to die from happiness.

★ ★ ★

Half an hour later, I went outside and found
Grace and Alice sitting on the garden wall,
waiting for me. I walked slowly towards them.

'Your mum's visit wasn't an accident, was it,
Alice?' I said. 'You told her to come and say
those nice things to Mum and Dad, didn't you?'

She grinned. 'Sort of.'

'Come on, Megan,' said Grace. 'Don't keep
us in suspense. Did it work?'

'Totally,' I said. 'I'm going to Lanzarote! My
mum has phoned your mum already, Grace,
and she's booked the flight and everything, and
it's all sorted, and I'm going. I'm really, really,
really going!'

Grace and Alice got down from the wall, and
we hugged and laughed and jumped up and
down, and everything was perfect.

Chapter Six

Five days later, Grace, Alice and I were sitting in the back of a shiny white minibus. In the seat in front of us were Grace's parents, Lorna and Eddie, and her big brother Gavin. Everyone except Gavin was chatting and laughing. All through the journey he'd been staring at his phone and looking like he was going to burst into tears. I felt sorry for him, and wondered why he was so sad.

Already, we'd passed tons of beaches, a volcano, a camel farm and all kinds of cool stuff. The others might have been tired of me saying 'Omigod!' over and over again, but I couldn't help it. This was the best place ever.

Soon we stopped at a huge red gate. There was a big sign on the pillar – *Sunset Beach Villas*.

'Here we are,' said Lorna, turning back and smiling at us. 'Home, sweet home.'

'Omigod,' I whispered. Everyone except Gavin laughed, and even he smiled a bit.

The minibus driver, José, leaned out through the minibus window and typed a code into a panel at the side of the gate. A second later, the gate swung open and we drove through, following a wide, curvy road. I stared out the window, all buzzy with excitement, as we passed rows of shiny white villas, and a kid-dies playground and a few really fancy-looking restaurants.

'There's the communal pool,' said Grace, pointing at the biggest swimming pool I'd ever seen. 'And the crazy golf course is just down there past the trees. We go to the communal pool sometimes, but most days we just hang out at our own pool.'

At last I was speechless. I couldn't even say

'Omigod' any more. This had to be the best place in the whole wide world.

We went past the pool, and through some trees. Then José drove down a narrow road, up a hill, and past more trees.

'Where are we going?' wailed Alice. 'I liked that place. Why are we leaving already?'

Eddie turned around and laughed. 'Our house is just up here,' he said. 'It's all on its own. It's nice and private and far from all the action.'

'Boring,' said Grace, rolling her eyes.

'We like it that way,' said Eddie. 'But if it's not exciting enough for you girls, you can go to the communal pool or the crazy golf whenever you want. In fact, as long as you stay within the complex, you can safely go pretty much wherever you like.'

By now, we were pulling up outside a huge white villa. Everyone climbed out of the mini-bus. José helped to unload the bags and then he drove away.

We stood on the terrace and looked around.

The air was warm and there was a smell of flowers and sea and holidays. In front of us, the swimming pool was all cool and sparkly.

'It's that time again,' said Lorna, smiling at us.

'What time?' asked Alice.

Instead of answering, Grace smiled too. 'Put your phones on the table,' she said.

I didn't like where this was going. Were Grace's parents going to take our phones from us? Even though I had hardly any credit, and I was only supposed to use my phone to talk to Mum and Dad every night, I didn't like the idea of being parted from it.

'But ...' began Alice.

'Just do it,' said Grace. 'It's tradition. We do this every time we have new visitors to our house.'

It sounded kind of weird, but I guessed if I didn't go along with Grace's family's tradition, I might never be asked to go on holidays with them again. I soooo didn't like the idea of that, so I copied everyone else. I pulled my phone out of my pocket and put it on the table. Lorna took off her expensive-looking jacket, and put it over a chair. Eddie and Gavin took off their watches.

'Now take off your shoes and stand at the edge of the pool,' said Grace. 'Over here, next to me.'

At last I thought I could see where this was going. We had our clothes on, but no one seemed to care. This was all mad and crazy and fun.

'One, two…..' said Eddie.

As he said 'three' everyone jumped in to the pool. I hesitated for a second, but Grace grabbed me and pulled me in with her. I just had time to take a breath before the beautiful cool water wrapped itself around me. We all came to the surface together, and everyone was splashing and laughing, even Gavin.

'Welcome to Lanzarote,' said Lorna.

I wiped the water from my face. 'Omigod,' I said. 'I totally love this place. Omigod.'

★ ★ ★

'Come on,' said Grace when we'd dried off a bit. 'I want to show you our room. We've got the best one, right at the top of the house.'

We followed her into a cool marble hall, and up two flights of polished wooden stairs.

'Ta-da,' said Grace as she flung the bedroom door open.

'Wow!' said Alice and I together.

It was the most amazing room I'd ever been in. It was like something out of a movie. Every surface was white and shiny. There were three beds, all covered with snowy white sheets. The huge windows were open and floaty white curtains fluttered in the breeze.

'There's even a balcony,' said Alice, stepping through the doorway. 'If Romeo shows up, I'm totally ready.'

I followed her onto the balcony and leaned on the railings. Far away, over the trees, I could see the sea sparkling in the sunshine. The balcony was huge and there was a big swinging couch at one end. I threw myself onto the couch, and closed my eyes. I thought that maybe I'd be very happy to spend the entire holiday lying there, swaying gently in the breeze.

Alice had gone back inside though, and a second later I heard a loud screech.

'OMG, Megan. Come here. Quickly.'

I jumped up and ran inside, afraid that something terrible had happened.

'What is it, Alice?' I asked. 'What's wrong?'

'OMG,' she said again. 'Have you ever seen a bathroom as big as this?'

★ ★ ★

When Alice and I had finished admiring everything, the three of us unpacked. Then we lay on the beds and looked at the ceiling fan circling slowly over our heads.

'No offence, Grace,' said Alice after a while.

'But your brother isn't the happiest guy I've ever met in my life.'

Grace sighed. 'He's not always like that,' she said. 'Usually he's great fun, but his girlfriend broke up with him and he's kind of gone to pieces.'

'The poor boy,' I said. 'That's so sad.'

Grace rolled her eyes. 'It's been nearly two weeks,' she said. 'He should be over it by now, and anyway, he had a lucky escape. His girlfriend, Leah, was a total witch.'

I laughed. 'Why?'

'Well she always called me "kiddo", for one thing, like she was all grown up, and I was just a baby. And she called him "Gavvy", which is just pathetic. And when she was around, Gavin was different – like everything he did had to please her. She made him cut his hair, and she tried to scare away his friends.'

'That's evil,' said Alice. 'Everyone needs friends.'

'I agree,' said Grace. 'But I haven't got to the

worst part yet. You see, it's not the first time Leah's broken up with Gavin. She's done it at least three times before. Each time, just as he's starting to get over it, she bounces back into his life and messes him up all over again.'

'Ouch,' I said. 'She sounds kind of mean all right. Pity he's so sad though.'

Grace sighed. 'He's a mess. I bet he's in his room right now, listening to sad songs, and looking at pictures of Leah on Facebook. That girl is so totally mean. Every time they break up, she posts pictures of herself hanging out with other guys and having a great time at parties. Gav can't help looking at the pictures and then he gets really upset.'

Alice sat up suddenly. Her eyes were all bright and sparkly. 'That's not healthy,' she said. 'We've got to fix him. We've got to help him to get over the witch lady.'

'Gavin's nineteen,' said Grace. 'He's grown-up. He doesn't need us to help him.'

I smiled to myself. Grace doesn't know

my best friend as well as I do. Alice had that dangerous look in her eyes, and she was on a mission. Nothing was going to stop her now.

Chapter Seven

Next morning, after a totally delicious and porridge-free breakfast, Grace, Alice and I put on our bikinis and went to lie outside in the sunshine.

I took out a monster-sized bottle of factor 50 sunscreen and started to rub it all over my arms and legs.

'Your mum?' asked Alice.

I nodded. 'If I go home with the tiniest trace of sunburn, she'll go crazy and she'll never let me out of her sight again – and I'm sooo not going to let that happen.'

'Anyway,' said Alice quickly. 'Enough about your mum. We've got more important things to worry about. We need to get started on our plan.'

'We have a plan?' asked Grace.

I giggled. 'Alice always has a plan,' I said. 'Don't bother arguing, because you'll end up doing what she wants anyway.'

Alice ignored me. 'Where's Gavin gone, Grace?'

Grace pointed to an open window at the side of the house. 'Can't you hear the sad music?' she said.

'That's why we need a plan,' said Alice. 'Music that sad can't be healthy. Anyway, the first problem is the way Gavin spends time looking at photographs of Witch-girl. Did you see him at breakfast-time?' He looked like he wanted to climb into the phone and hug her. He'll never get over her while he's doing that.'

'That's true,' said Grace. 'But how do you suggest we stop him?'

'Could you tease him until he gets really mad, and then your mum and dad could take his phone from him?' I suggested. 'My parents are forever doing that to me when I get mad at Rosie.'

Grace and Alice both laughed, which was a bit mean. 'He's nineteen,' said Grace. 'I think he's a bit old to be banned from his phone.'

She was right of course, and that made me feel worse.

'I know,' said Alice. 'I could "accidentally" push Gavin into the pool while he's got his phone in his hand.'

I rolled my eyes. Trust Alice to go for the dramatic option.

'No way!' said Grace. 'He just got that phone last week and it was really, really expensive. If it goes for an "accidental" swim, Gav will go crazy. We need to find a way of stopping him from checking up on Witch-girl, without actually damaging his phone.'

'OMG!' I said. 'I know what to do. My mum threatened to do it to me last week when she caught me on the computer when I was supposed to be doing my homework. One of her loser-hippy friends told her about a way of blocking access to particular sites.'

'Yesss!' said Alice. 'Good idea, Meg. Only thing is if we block Gavin's phone, he'll probably find another way of getting on the internet. Is there a computer in the house, Grace?'

Grace grinned. 'No. There are no computers or laptops here. Mum and Dad wanted this house to be kind of a computer-free haven. They don't bring their smartphones with them either. If we block Gavin's phone, he won't have any other way of getting on to a site to gaze at his lost love.'

'Sounds good,' I said. 'Except for one small detail.'

'Which is?' asked Alice.

'How are we going to get at Gavin's phone?' I asked. 'He always has it in his hand. I haven't seen him put it down since we got here.'

'I heard him saying he was going for a run this morning,' said Grace. 'He'll bring his phone with him, of course – he always does.

But after the run, he'll have a shower, and even *he* doesn't bring his phone into the shower with him. Hopefully he'll leave it in his bedroom and we'll be able to get it then.'

'We won't have much time though,' I said.

Grace laughed. 'We'll have *ages*,' she said. 'Gavin always has really, really long showers – Mum and Dad kill him for using so much hot water. Trust me, we'll have plenty of time to do whatever we want to his phone.'

'Perfect,' said Alice. 'That's when we'll do it. Get ready, girls, step one will be happening very soon.'

★ ★ ★

An hour later, I was standing guard outside the bathroom, and Grace was at Gavin's bedroom door, waiting for a signal from me. Inside the bedroom, Alice was madly trying to figure out how to block all social media sites from Gavin's phone. She's really good at computers and stuff, but still, I was all nervous and jumpy.

Much too soon, I heard the sound of the shower being turned off.

'Quickly,' I whispered to Grace. 'Tell Alice to finish up. He's going to be out any second.'

Grace nodded and passed on the message.

From the bathroom, I could hear the shower door opening and closing. Then there was the sound of a towel being pulled from a rail. Gavin was whistling the chorus of a sad love song. I felt a bit mean listening to him, but mostly I felt terrified.

What was I going to do if Gavin came out, before Alice was finished?

How was I going to stop him from going into his bedroom?

Was it going to be totally embarrassing if I had to stand on the landing with him while he was only wearing a towel?

I heard the sound of bare feet on tiles.

'Quick,' I hissed. 'He's coming. He's coming.'

For a second, nothing happened. I heard the

rattle of the key in the bathroom door. I wondered if I should throw myself on the floor and pretend to be dying. I mightn't even have to fake it. I actually felt like I was going to die.

And then, at the very last second, Alice came racing out of Gavin's room. She slammed the door behind her, just as Gavin opened the bathroom door.

'Hey, Gav,' said Alice breathlessly. 'How's it going? Did you have a nice shower?'

And before the poor boy had time to answer, Grace, Alice and I raced up the stairs to our room. My heart was all jumpy, and I thought I was going to faint. Alice was laughing though. She loves danger.

She threw herself onto her bed and sighed. 'Phew, that was close,' she said. 'But the good news is, it's done. I've blocked Gavin from every site he's been on in the past week – and that's pretty much every social media site in the world.'

Even though the whole thing had been my

idea, now that Alice had actually done it, it seemed kind of extreme.

'Is Gavin's phone going to stay like that forever?' I asked.

'Nah,' said Alice. 'I could easily have blocked him forever, but that might have been a bit mean.'

'So what happens?' asked .Grace.

'He'll be automatically unblocked after five days,' said Alice. 'And hopefully, by then he'll have forgotten all about Leah.'

I smiled. 'The wicked witch will just be a distant memory. Well done, Alice. I think this is really going to work.'

★   ★   ★

When Gavin came down for lunch, he had his phone in his hand as usual.

'He doesn't look happy,' whispered Alice.

'No change there, then,' said Grace. 'He hasn't been happy for weeks.'

'Everything OK, Gav?' asked Lorna.

'No,' he said. 'It's not OK. It's a disaster. There's something wrong with my phone. It won't let me go on to any of my usual sites.'

'Let's have a look,' said Alice, winking at Grace and me. 'I'm good with phones. Maybe I can figure out what's wrong.'

'Look,' he said, as he handed the phone to Alice. 'I've tried all my favourite sites, and the same message keeps popping up – *This website is blocked.*'

Alice pressed a few buttons, managing to look like she was trying to help. 'Oh, dear,' she said in the end. 'You probably have a virus.'

'That doesn't sound like a virus to me,' said Lorna.

I agreed with her, but Alice just smiled at Gavin. 'It's a new virus,' she said. 'And that's probably why you haven't heard of it. I only know about it because my dad got it on his phone a few weeks ago.'

'And how did he fix it?' asked Gavin, taking

the phone back from her.

Alice pretended to think. 'Hmmm,' she said. 'Oh, yes. I remember now. He took it to an expert and he said it was one of those things that usually fixes itself after a while.'

'After how long?' asked Gavin.

'Oh,' said Alice. 'I can't really remember. I think my dad's phone was OK after a few days, or maybe a week or something.'

Gavin looked at her with wild, scared eyes, like she'd told him the virus was going to last for a hundred years.

'Anyway,' said Eddie. 'Lunch is ready now. Why don't you leave the phone down, Gavin, and engage with the outside world for a bit?'

And, amazingly, that's what Gavin did. Lorna brought out some cold drinks, and Eddie served us really delicious bowls of pasta, and Gavin put the phone down, and chatted to us, and he was really quite sweet and funny, and Alice grinned at me, and I remembered once again how very, very good she is at sorting things out.

Chapter Eight

After lunch, Gavin went upstairs, Lorna and Eddie went to play tennis, and Grace, Alice and I went back to our sunloungers.

'That was a great idea,' said Grace. 'I'm glad you two were able to fix things for Gavin.'

'Hey,' said Alice. 'We're not finished yet. That was only the beginning. We've got lots more to do.'

'Like what?' I asked.

'Well,' said Alice. 'Clearly Gavin doesn't feel good about himself.'

'Why do you say that?' asked Grace.

'Because if he felt good about himself, he wouldn't have let that awful Leah person treat him so badly,' said Alice.

'And now that she's dumped him again, he must feel even worse,' I said.

'Exactly,' said Alice. 'So our next job is to make him feel better about himself. As soon as we've managed that, we'll find a nice girl and get them together. It's time he moved on.'

'Hey,' said Grace. 'Hang on a sec, Alice. Don't you think you're getting a bit carried away here?'

'No,' said Alice.

'You're just going to find some randomer, and hope that Gavin falls in love with her?' asked Grace.

'Sure,' said Alice. 'And anyway, don't forget that everyone in the world is a randomer until you get to know them.'

Grace was looking at Alice like she should argue with her, but I shook my head, warning her that she'd only be wasting her time.

'Let's worry about the love story of the century later,' I said. 'Before we get to that, we've got to make Gavin feel better about himself. How do you suggest we do that, Alice? Are we all supposed to sit around taking turns saying nice stuff about him?'

'That's a brilliant idea,' said Alice.

I'd only been joking, but I like when Alice goes with one of my ideas, so I didn't argue.

'Gavin's up in his room,' said Grace. 'And there's no way I'm sitting on the landing saying nice stuff to him through his bedroom door. That's just weird.'

'And I want to sunbathe,' I added.

'Calm down, you two,' she said. 'I'm not suggesting that we stalk the poor boy. That *would* be crazy. We can take the afternoon off to catch some rays, but at dinner-time, we have to get going on part two of the plan. Everyone has to help, so I expect you two to have lots of good things ready to say about Gavin. OK?'

Grace and I nodded obediently.

'Yes, Boss,' I said. 'Whatever you say, Boss.'

Alice rolled her eyes. 'Sometimes you are sooo immature, Megan,' she said.

Whatever,' I said. 'Now pass me my sun-cream, I'm wasting precious sunbathing time.'

★ ★ ★

That evening, when we were sitting enjoying the delicious barbecue that Eddie had prepared, Alice went into action.

'Hey, Gavin,' she said. 'I totally love that shirt you're wearing – and those shoes are great. What do you think, Megan? Doesn't Gavin look well tonight?'

The table was lit by lots of flickery candles, and I hoped that no one could see how red my face had gone. As usual, Alice was going completely over the top. Also, I was kind of starting to think that Gavin looked really well all of the time, and there was *no* way I wanted anyone to know about that.

Alice wasn't happy with my silence. 'Hello? Megan? Don't you think Gavin looks great tonight?'

'Er, yes, I guess he does,' I said, not looking up from my dinner.

'And your hair is totally cool, Gavin,' said Alice. 'I love the way the sun has started to bleach it at the ends. You look like a Californian surfer or something.'

Eddie gave a sarcastic laugh. 'It would be a miracle if the sun managed to bleach Gavin's hair. We've barely been in Lanzarote twenty-four hours, and Gavin has spent most of that time in his bedroom.'

I'd have been embarrassed, but Alice wasn't even listening to what he said.

She turned to Grace. 'What's your favourite thing about your brother?' she asked. Grace hesitated, and then I saw Alice kick her under the table. I felt sorry for her. Alice's kicks are usually kind of painful.

'Er ...' said Grace, 'I guess he ... well ... he ...

he's … he's funny. He's good at telling jokes and … stuff …'

That was fairly pathetic, but Alice didn't seem to notice.

She turned to Lorna. 'What's your favourite thing about Gavin?' she asked.

Lorna leaned over and put her arm around Gavin. 'He's my son,' she said. 'And I think every single thing about him is perfect.'

Grace rolled her eyes and pretended to vomit into her serviette. Before anyone else could say anything, Alice turned to Eddie. 'What about you?' she asked. 'What's your favourite thing about Gavin?'

Eddie looked up from his dinner and stared at Alice. 'That's easy,' he said. 'I think my favourite thing about Gavin is that he doesn't keep on and on asking stupid questions while I'm trying to enjoy my food.'

Ouch. That was direct enough, even for Alice.

'I'm just trying to make conversation,' she

muttered. 'Is there a law against that in Lan-zarote? And would someone mind passing me the salad?'

Gavin picked up the salad bowl and passed it to her. She smiled at him, like he'd just given her a bowl full of diamonds. 'Thank you so, so much, Gavin,' she said. 'You're always really, really helpful.'

Lorna gave Alice a funny look. 'What's going on?' she asked. 'Is this an official "be-kind-to-Gavin" night?'

This was a bit close to the truth, and I hoped it was the kind of question that didn't expect an answer. Alice suddenly seemed very inter-ested in cutting up her steak, and Grace started to tear her serviette into tiny shreds.

Suddenly Gavin stood up. Alice had done her best, but he didn't look like he felt better about himself. Mostly he just looked embar-rassed, which wasn't really part of the plan.

'I'm finished my dinner,' he said. 'And I'm kind of tired. May I be excused?'

'Of course you may,' said Lorna. 'Good night, and sleep well.'

As soon as Gavin had gone inside, Alice leaned over to me. 'OK, so maybe that wasn't a huge success,' she whispered. 'But don't worry. Tomorrow's another day, and we've got the whole night to come up with a bigger, better plan.'

Chapter Nine

When I woke up the next morning, Alice was sitting on the end of my bed, grinning.

'What?' I asked, rubbing my eyes.

'I've been awake for ages,' she said. 'And I've got a brilliant plan to make Gavin feel good about himself.'

'What is it?' asked Grace, sitting up in bed. 'It needs to be good, because, no offence, Alice, last night's plan was a bit of a disaster.'

'I've already forgotten about last night,' said Alice primly. 'The past is past – and today's plan is perfect.'

'What is it?' I said, half afraid to hear the

answer. Alice's plans are never boring, but often they are totally, totally crazy.

'The new plan is simple, but effective,' said Alice. 'I've realised that saying nice stuff about people is a bit weird, especially if you do it all in a rush, like we did.'

Grace giggled. 'It took you the whole night to figure that out?' she asked.

Alice ignored her. 'I've just remembered a really interesting article I read in a magazine last year.'

'Do share,' I said.

'The article was about six pages long,' she said. 'And I got bored and stopped reading halfway through it, but the basic point was that helping people makes you feel good about yourself.'

'That's probably true,' I said. 'I felt really good about myself when I helped Rosie to cycle her bike without stabilisers. And for weeks after-wards, every time I saw her on her bike, I felt all warm and happy.'

'So sweet,' said Grace. 'And I see where you're going with this, Alice, but there's one problem. Who around here needs help?'

'Oh don't you worry about that,' said Alice. 'Leave it to me. I've got it all figured out.'

'What are you going to do?' I asked.

'I'll tell you when the time is right,' said Alice. 'I'm working on a need-to-know basis, and for now, I'm the only one who needs to know. Now who's coming down for breakfast? I'm starving.'

I should have known to be afraid.

★ ★ ★

After breakfast, Lorna and Eddie went shopping. When the rest of us had tidied the kitchen, Gavin went upstairs as usual and Alice, Grace and I went to lie beside the pool.

'Poor Gavin,' I said as we settled down on our sunloungers. 'Can you hear that sad music coming from his room again? He's playing the same few songs over and over again. A broken heart must really hurt.'

Alice jumped up from her sunlounger, and I suddenly remembered the plan she hadn't shared with us.

'You're right, Megan,' she said. 'A broken heart must be awful. We can't waste any more time. We need to move on to the next stage of our plan.'

She walked across the patio until she was standing right under Gavin's window. She grinned at Grace and me, and then she took a deep breath. 'Er, Alice,' I said nervously. 'What exactly are you——?'

Before I could finish my sentence, she screamed loudly. 'Gavin!!'

When my ears had finally recovered, I noticed that the sad music had stopped. A second later, Gavin leaned out of the window. Even from a distance I could see how sad his huge brown eyes were. He looked like a big, lost puppy.

'What do you want?' he asked. 'Why are you

calling me?'

'We need your help,' said Alice sweetly. 'Grace told me before that you're a really good swimmer.'

'Er ... I suppose I'm not too bad,' he said. 'But how is that going to help you? It doesn't look like you're drowning or anything.'

'Ha, ha,' said Alice. 'That's really funny, Gavin. The problem is – Megan can't swim.'

'Alice!' I hissed, but she ignored me and continued. 'So we thought maybe you could give her a lesson.'

'Oh,' said Gavin, looking surprised. 'Would you like that, Megan?'

I could feel my face going red, and before I could answer, Alice answered for me.

'Of course she'd like it. She's just a bit shy, that's all. You'd love a swimming lesson from Gavin, wouldn't you, Megan?'

I was totally, totally embarrassed. I felt sorry for Gavin too, though, so I didn't argue. I put my hands over my red face and half-nodded.

'OK,' said Gavin. 'I'll be down in a sec.' And then he vanished from the window.

'That's totally unfair, Alice,' I said as soon as he was gone. 'You know I don't need a swimming lesson. I can swim perfectly well already – better than you.'

'You can pretend, can't you?' said Alice. 'It's all in a good cause. Don't you want to help Gavin?'

'But I've just finished putting on my sunscreen.'

Alice picked up the bottle and read from the label on the back. '100 per cent waterproof. I knew we could rely on Sheila. You can swim all you want, Megan. Isn't that lucky?'

Grace giggled, but stopped when I glared at her.

'This is totally stupid,' I said. 'Why didn't you say …?'

Before I could finish, Gavin appeared. There was no way I was letting him think I was a total idiot, so I tried to smile.

'Er, thanks for coming down, Gavin,' I said. 'But Alice got a bit mixed up – she does that sometimes. But the thing is – I can actually swim.'

'So you don't need my help?' he asked, looking surprised.

I was about to agree with him, when I saw Alice glaring at me. I suddenly remembered that she wasn't deliberately embarrassing me. In her usual OTT way, she was trying to be nice.

'I do ... kind of need your help, Gavin,' I said. 'It's just maybe ... you know ... you could give me a few pointers ... you know ... to improve my stroke and stuff.'

'Sure thing,' said Gavin. 'I can easily do that. Why don't you swim a length or two and we'll see what needs to be done?'

So I climbed into the pool, and swam up and down a few times. It was totally embarrassing, knowing that the others were all watching me, but there wasn't a whole lot I could do about it.

When I stopped swimming, Gavin sat at the

edge of the pool. I concentrated on his big brown eyes, and did my best to ignore Alice and Grace, who were making faces at me behind his back.

'You could be a really nice swimmer if you just tweaked a few things,' he said. 'Your kick is a bit off, and if we fix that, you'll see a huge improvement.'

'Thanks,' I said. 'I'd like to do that.'

'Well let's get started then,' said Gavin, and he gave me a big smile, that made me feel kind of embarrassed and happy at the same time.

Gavin was really, really patient. He explained things carefully, and encouraged me when I got it right. After a bit, he took off his t-shirt and got into the pool to demonstrate what he'd been describing. Alice was still watching, but she wasn't making faces any more. I got the weird feeling that she was a bit jealous. I grinned and waved at her, and she sat back on her sunlounger and pretended to read her book.

After half an hour, Gavin climbed out of the pool. 'You did really well, Megan,' he said. 'I can give you another lesson tomorrow if you like.'

'I'd love that,' I said, grabbing a towel and rubbing it through my hair, so he wouldn't see how embarrassed I was.

When I'd finished drying my hair, he was gone, and from inside the house I could hear the sad music starting up again.

'OMG,' said Grace. 'That plan totally worked. Did you see how much Gavin smiled while he was teaching Megan? I bet he didn't think about evil witch-woman the whole time. You're a genius, Alice.'

'Thanks,' said Alice. 'But I knew that already. We're not finished with Gavin yet, though – he's still playing that awful music. Now be quiet, so I can think of a plan for tomorrow.'

★ ★ ★

After lunch, Grace showed us these cool motor-scooter things we were allowed to use, and we spent ages driving around the villa complex, checking everything out. Then we did more sunbathing, and I practised my swimming and Lorna and Eddie prepared for a barbecue.

Mum rang just as we were getting ready to eat. It was nice to hear her voice, but it quickly turned into a question and answer session.

'Did you remember to put on your sunscreen?'

'Did you make sure not to swim until an hour after eating?'

'Did you help Lorna and Eddie with the dishes?'

'Are you avoiding sweets and biscuits?'

'Are you eating plenty of fruit and vegetables?'

'Are you drinking plenty of water?'

My answer was always the same. 'Yes, Mum. Yes, Mum. Yes, Mum.' It was like I was singing the chorus of a very boring song.

In the end, I couldn't take any more. 'Er, Mum, it's lovely to talk to you,' I said. 'But I need to go. We're having a barbecue and I think it might be ready.'

That was a mistake. A big mistake. My innocent excuse set off a whole new string of commandments.

'Don't stand too near the barbecue.'

'I'm sure Lorna and Eddie are very careful, but make sure you don't eat any pink chicken.'

'Burned food is very bad for you, so be careful not too eat anything that's too black.'

'Mum,' I said impatiently. 'I really need to go. Everyone's waiting for me.'

Her voice went all soft and mushy and I felt sorry. 'OK, darling,' she said. 'We love you and we miss you. Rosie and Dad and Domino send hugs and kisses and cuddles.'

'Bye, Mum,' I love you too,' I said, and then I hung up.

Later I managed not to get burned or poisoned by the barbecue, and then we went to bed and that was the end of our first full day in Lanzarote.

Chapter Ten

The next morning, Gavin gave me another swimming lesson. Once again he was really nice and helpful. Once again, Alice sat by the pool, pretending not to watch, pretending she didn't mind that I was the one getting all the attention.

'Watch out, Megan,' she said after a bit. 'Or before you know it, you'll end up at the Olympic games.'

'She very well might,' said Gavin. 'She's good enough.' And I had to dive quickly under the water so he wouldn't see how red my face had gone.

When my lesson was over, and Gavin had

gone back inside, Alice, Grace and I decided to check out the communal pool. We picked three sunloungers near the snack bar, right in the middle of the action.

'OK,' said Alice, as soon as I had got comfortable. 'We've got work to do.'

'Work,' I wailed. 'Aren't we supposed to be on holidays? What work do we have to do?'

'It's time for us to find a nice girl for Gavin,' said Alice.

'Maybe he doesn't want a girl, nice or otherwise,' said Grace. 'Maybe he just wants a quiet life.'

'A quiet life isn't an option when Alice is around,' I said giggling. 'Haven't you figured that out yet?'

'But what if—?' began Grace before Alice interrupted her.

'Hey,' she said. 'What about that girl over there?'

She was pointing at a blonde girl who was lying at the other side of the pool.

'Well, she's very pretty, and she looks about the right age for Gavin,' I said. 'What do you think, Grace? You're the one who should decide. Remember the girl we pick might one day be your sister-in-law.'

Before Grace could answer, a boy came and sat down next to the blonde girl. He leaned over and gave her a big smoochy kiss.

'Good choice, Alice,' said Grace.

'Oh, well,' said Alice. 'You win some you lose some. Now what about that girl coming out of the snack bar?'

★ ★ ★

For the next half hour, Alice picked out lots of girls and Grace and I rejected them for one reason or another. Grace said no to one girl, just because she didn't like her swimsuit. I said no to another girl because she reminded me a bit of Melissa. I felt a small bit guilty, judging all these strangers, but I didn't say anything because it was also great fun.

We were just thinking about going back to the villa, when a girl came and put her towel down on a sunlounger near us. She was tall, with long dark hair. She wasn't exactly pretty, but she looked nice, like she'd be kind to puppies and small kids and stuff. As she sat down, she looked at us, and smiled for a second, but when her smile faded, her eyes seemed sad. Then she opened her book and started to read.

'OMG!' mouthed Alice to Grace and me. 'She's the one.'

Suddenly I felt nervous. I was totally afraid of what Alice was going to do next. My best friend has no idea how to be subtle.

I jumped up and started to roll up my towel.

'We should be going,' I said. 'It's nearly time for ... dinner ... or ... lunch ... or our nap ... or something.'

Grace took the hint, and she stood up too and started to get ready to leave. Alice wasn't giving up though. She stood up and went over to the girl.

'It's a nice day, isn't it?' she said, which I thought was a bit pathetic. Who wants to talk about the weather? Especially in a country where nearly every day is nice?

The girl was polite though. She smiled at Alice and nodded.

'Is that a good book?' asked Alice.

The girl smiled and nodded again, but she had a puzzled look on her face. I guess she was wondering why this stranger kept asking her stupid questions. I couldn't bear to watch any more.

'I'm going back to the villa,' I said. 'Anyone coming?'

Alice pretended not to hear, so Grace and I walked towards the exit, and waited. And waited.

We watched as Alice sat on the end of the girl's sunlounger, like they were best friends.

We watched as the girl put her book down and said something to Alice.

We watched as Alice laughed like the girl had just told her the funniest joke in the universe.

Then we waited some more.

In the end I had to go back. I felt sorry for the girl who might one day be Grace's sister-in-law.

'Come on, Alice,' I said. 'It's getting late. We really, really need to go now.'

'Bye, Robyn,' said Alice, as if it was perfectly normal to have your friend pulling your arm and practically dragging you along the edge of a swimming pool. 'Maybe I'll see you here tomorrow?'

'Sure,' said the girl. 'I guess I'll be here.'

'She's perfect,' said Alice as we walked back to Grace. 'Totally perfect. She's really nice and friendly, but not totally vain and prissy like some girls her age are. And best of all – she hasn't got a boyfriend.'

'You asked her?' That was brave even for Alice.

'Not exactly,' said Alice. 'I just said that I'd love

to have a boyfriend, and she said I shouldn't be in any hurry about that. She said her boyfriend broke up with her three weeks ago.'

'Aw, that's kind of sweet,' I said. 'Maybe she and Gavin can be sad together.'

'And then they can get over it all, and be happy together,' said Grace, sounding enthusiastic about the plan for the first time.

'Anyway,' said Alice, 'Her name's Robyn. Her dad is English and her mum is Spanish – that's probably where she gets her dark skin from. She lives in England, but she comes here for a few weeks every year.'

'Funny I've never seen her before,' said Grace. 'We've been coming here since I was tiny.'

'It's fate,' sighed Alice. 'Fate kept her and Gavin apart until the perfect moment – which is like, now.'

'Or maybe they never met before because they get different school holidays in England?' I said.

'Anyway,' said Alice, who always prefers

exotic explanations to likely ones. 'Who cares why they never met before? The important thing is that they are going to meet now.'

'So what else did you find out about my future sister-in-law?' asked Grace.

It turned out Alice had found out a lot – especially considering she'd only had about five minutes to do it.

'Well, she goes to college in London. She's in first year, same as Gavin. She hasn't got any brothers or sisters, and usually she brings a friend on holidays with her, but this time she asked her boyfriend to come, and when he broke up with her, it was too late to ask anyone else, so now it's just her and her parents. She says it's a bit boring.'

'Oh, well,' I said, giggling. 'I'm sure we can rely on you to give her a holiday she'll never forget.'

'Thanks, Meg,' said Alice. 'Good to know you've got so much confidence in me. Now I'm starving after all that hard work. Let's get some lunch, and then we can start to properly plan the romance of the century.'

★ ★ ★

After lunch, Gavin went for a run, so Alice, Grace and I were free to discuss our plans for the rest of his life.

'Robyn told me she's going out with her parents this afternoon, and she won't be back till late tonight,' said Alice. 'That means we can't make a move until tomorrow morning.'

'And what exactly are we going to do?' asked Grace.

'Not much, really,' said Alice. 'We've just got to get Gavin to go to the communal pool, and then we've got to make sure that Robyn notices him.'

'Getting him there won't be a problem,' I said. 'He told me this morning that it would be easier to improve my swimming strokes in a bigger pool. I'll just ask him to come with me and give me a lesson there.'

'Great,' said Alice. 'Good idea, Meg. Now, I've got a few suggestions for getting Robyn to notice Gavin. How about we secretly write a totally embarrassing message on the back of his t-shirt while he's in the shower? Robyn could see it and feel sorry for him. Or we could swap his shower gel for hair removal cream, and when he's going crazy wondering why his legs aren't hairy any more, Robyn might ask him what's wrong. Or we could unscrew the leg of his sunlounger, and when he sits down it'll collapse, and Robyn could help him to get up. Or we could—'

'Hey,' I said holding up my hands. 'How about you stop right there?'

Alice looked surprised, and actually stopped talking.

'I know you're trying to help and every-thing,' I said. 'But why do you always have to be so extreme? Why don't we just get Gavin to the pool, and hope that Robyn is there, and then, maybe they'll just start chatting to each other – like normal people do.'

Alice sighed. 'You're right as usual, Meg. I might have let myself get a teeny-tiny bit carried away. Let's try your idea first – but if it doesn't work, we're going for the extreme stuff, OK?'

'OK,' I said. 'Deal. And let's just hope that Gavin never has to find out exactly how extreme you can be.'

Chapter Eleven

The next morning, Gavin seemed happier than I'd ever seen him – which wouldn't really have been all that hard. There was no sad music playing in his bedroom, and his still-blocked phone was nowhere to be seen.

'Maybe he's cured,' I said to Alice as we went upstairs to brush our teeth after breakfast. 'Maybe we've done enough. Maybe we can let him sort out his own love-life.'

'No way,' said Alice. 'We're just getting started.'

I sighed. Alice loves plotting and scheming.

Even if Gavin was the happiest guy on the planet by now, she still wouldn't want to pull back.

'I think Alice is right,' said Grace. 'We have to make sure Gavin is fully better. If we stop too soon, there's a danger he'll go crawling back to Witch-girl – and I soooo don't want *her* back in our lives.'

'OK,' I said. 'You both win. I know what I've got to do.'

When we went back downstairs, Gavin was sitting in the kitchen.

'Hey, Megan,' he said when he saw me. 'Ready for today's lesson?'

'Hey, Gavin,' I said. 'Do you think you could come with us to the communal pool and give me my lesson there? Remember you said that would be better for my strokes?'

'Sure,' he said. 'Good idea. I'll go get my towel and stuff.'

'Take your time,' said Alice sweetly. 'We'll go on ahead and find a nice place for us all to sit.'

As we walked over to the communal pool, I started to feel guilty.

'Robyn seems like a really nice girl,' I said.

'Yeah,' said Grace. 'I agree.'

'But in a way that makes it worse,' I said.

'Makes what worse?' asked Alice.

'We're messing around with Robyn's life to help someone else,' I said. 'Basically we're using her.'

'And the problem is?' asked Alice. 'It's all in a good cause, isn't it?'

'Alice, don't you remember what happened when we tried to set your dad up with my Aunt Linda?' I asked.

'I laughed so much when you told me that story,' said Grace. 'I wish I could have been there to see it.'

'Yeah, well,' I sighed. 'It might have been funny, but Alice and I got in a *lot* of trouble over it. Mum and Dad were really cross with me, and the worst thing was, they were right. It *was* mean to use Linda to try to make Alice's

Mum jealous.'

'Ancient history,' said Alice. 'And I've always hated history. And anyway, this is completely different. Gavin and Robyn are young, not like Dad and Linda. And we shouldn't forget, if our plan works, Robyn will gain too. Gavin's a total catch. Those two could live happily ever after, and it will all be thanks to us. We might even get to be bridesmaids at their wedding. What do you think, would pink dresses suit all three of us, or would green be nicer?'

We were at the pool by now, so I couldn't argue any more.

I wasn't sure if I was happy to see Robyn sitting in the same place as the day before.

Had she *any* idea of Alice's plans for the rest of her life?

What would she have thought if she knew that Alice was already planning what to wear to her wedding?

Alice grabbed three sunloungers, conveniently leaving an empty space between herself and Robyn. Robyn looked up from her book and smiled at us, and then we settled down to wait for Gavin.

After a few minutes, Alice nudged me.

'Oh, look, Meg,' she said, much too loudly. 'Here's Gavin. Wow, he looks good in those swimming shorts, doesn't he? He should be a male model or something.'

As usual, she was getting totally carried away. She was right though, he did look totally cool. I half-turned, and smiled when I saw that Robyn was peeping over the top of her book, and looking towards Gavin.

Alice poked me again. 'Up you get, Megan. It's time for your swimming lesson. Gavin is soooo kind to help you like this. I think he must be the kindest guy I've ever met in my whole life.'

Feeling like a complete idiot. I stood up and walked towards the pool. I felt like everyone was staring at me, and that so wasn't a good feeling.

As I jumped into the water, Gavin threw his towel onto the empty sunlounger next to Robyn. I rolled my eyes as Alice and Grace had a fit of winking and grinning at each other.

Then Gavin came and sat on the edge of the pool, and my lesson began.

It should have been totally embarrassing, having a public lesson like that, but after a few minutes, I almost forgot that anyone else was around. Gavin was really patient and encouraging, and soon I started to believe that I was the best swimmer in the world. Anytime I did something right, he smiled at me, and I felt like he'd given me a wonderful present, specially designed just for me.

I was really sorry when he stood up and stretched. 'That's probably enough for today, Megan,' he said. 'I don't want to confuse you by showing you too much new stuff. Practise what I showed you, and we'll continue tomorrow, OK?'

'OK,' I said. 'I'd like that.'

Suddenly I felt that if Gavin asked me to swim to America, I'd happily have done it for a single one of his crinkly smiles.

As I went to lie on my sunlounger, Gavin jumped into the pool and started to swim. He was a brilliant swimmer, and barely rippled the water as he sped along. I turned around and noticed that Robyn had put down her book, and was watching him too. When he stopped swimming, after about ten lengths, I felt a really stupid urge to start clapping, like he'd just won a gold medal or something. Luckily, I was sitting on my hands, so a disaster was averted.

When Gavin pulled himself out of the pool, Robyn quickly picked up her book again and looked totally interested in it. I smiled to myself when I saw that it was upside-down. I hoped no one else noticed.

Gavin picked up his towel. 'See you later, girls,' he said as he started to walk away.

'Hey,' called Alice. 'Come back.'

He turned around. 'What is it?' he asked. 'Is

something wrong?'

'No,' said Alice. 'Or, yes ... or maybe ... I mean ... you see ... there was this guy hanging around here earlier ... and I thought he was a bit creepy ... and he was staring at us ...'

'Where?' asked Gavin. 'Where is he? Maybe we should tell the lifeguard.'

'It *might* only be my imagination,' said Alice. 'But just in case, will you sit here with us for a bit? If the guy comes back, he'd be totally afraid of you.'

'OK,' said Gavin, as he sat down on the sun-lounger next to Robyn. 'Happy to protect my little sis and her friends.'

'Oh, said Alice, all casual. 'Robyn, this is Grace's brother Gavin.'

Robyn put her book down again and as they said 'hi' to each other, I noticed that they had both turned a bit red. I'm not an expert on boyfriend and girlfriend stuff, but I guessed that was a good sign. Nobody said anything for a minute. It wasn't exactly awkward, but I didn't like the look in Alice's eye. Was she considering something crazy like pushing them both into the pool?

Then, before Alice could do anything stupid, Gavin pointed at Robyn's book. 'Hey,' he said. 'I read that at college last term, and loved it. What do you think of it?'

Robyn smiled at him, and I realised that she was really pretty when she smiled. 'I totally love it,' she said. 'He's a great writer. What did you think of his book about Africa?'

'I liked it,' said Gavin. 'But not as much as this one. What did you think of the part where they go to Amsterdam? Wasn't it totally creepy?'

And that was all it took. Grace, Alice and I lay back on our sunloungers and closed our eyes, and pretended not to listen, while Gavin and Robyn discussed every book they'd ever read, and every one they hoped to read.

Sweet!

Chapter Twelve

The next few days were lovely. Gavin always found half an hour to give me a swimming lesson, and these were my favourite half-hours of the day. As I climbed out of the pool on the fourth day, he smiled at me.

'You're doing really well, Megan.' he said. 'You're a model pupil. You have a lovely stroke, and lots of stamina.'

'Oh,' I said. His praise was making me feel embarrassed, and my next words came out by accident. 'I think I might try out for the school swim team when I get back home.'

'That's a brilliant idea,' he said. 'You definitely should. You'd be great. Now I've got to go, Robyn's waiting.'

By now, Gavin spent most of his time with Robyn. They weren't all soppy and smoochy and kissy-kissy, but they just looked totally happy, like they belonged together.

Alice, Grace and I spent most of our time sunbathing, or swimming in one of the pools. Every night Eddie or Lorna cooked a delicious barbecue, and we ate out on the terrace, enjoying the warm air and the smell of holidays.

One morning I woke up and my first thought was – *I'm in this amazing place.*

My second thought was – *We've only got two days left.*

Why does time always have to go so quickly when you're having fun?

★ ★ ★

'Where's everyone?' asked Alice that lunch-time, when we got back after a brilliant game of mini-golf.

'I guess Gavin is off somewhere being romantic with Robyn,' said Grace, as she used her key to let us in. 'But I don't know where Mum and Dad could be. They went to play tennis, but they should be back here by now. Dad said he wanted to try out a new barbecue recipe for lunch.'

She didn't seem too worried, so I decided not to worry either. Grace got us each an ice-cream from the freezer and we lay by the pool for a while, enjoying the warm sunshine.

When Gavin came back an hour later, there was still no sign of Eddie and Lorna. He tried both their phones, but no one answered his mum's and we could hear the sound of his dad's phone ringing on the kitchen counter. Gavin was trying to act casual, but it wasn't really working. He sat on a sunlounger next to us for a few minutes, but he couldn't relax. He was all jumpy and nervous and he kept checking his watch.

'Relax, Gav,' said Grace after a while. 'Mum

and Dad are grown-ups. They don't have to tell us where they are every minute of every day. They've probably decided to go out for lunch or something.'

'But I wanted to see them before I go,' he said.

'You're going somewhere?' asked Grace. 'You never said.'

'Is it a romantic date with Robyn?' asked Alice. 'Maybe you should buy her flowers. Or you could "borrow" some from the villa at the end of this road. They've got heaps in their garden.'

He went red. 'Actually it's not really a date. It's more like I'm doing her a favour.'

'What kind of favour?' asked Alice. 'Are you going to rescue her from a dragon or something? That's totally romantic.'

I thought she was being kind of cheeky, but Gavin didn't seem to mind.

'It's not all that romantic,' he said. 'Robyn's Spanish cousins live on the other side of the island, and they're having a big family celebration tonight.'

'I'm not seeing the favour here,' said Alice.

'Well, when Robyn was a kid, her cousins bullied her a lot,' he said. 'There's seven of them, and they always ganged up on her. They used to tease her for her English accent, and her English ways.'

'That's really mean. Poor Robyn,' I said, thinking of how bad I feel when Melissa is around.

'Yeah,' said Gavin. 'It was rotten. Anyway, ages ago, Robyn told the mean cousins she'd be bringing her boyfriend to the party, and they made a big deal of it.'

'But now the boyfriend isn't around any more, and they're giving her a hard time?' said Grace.

'Exactly,' said Gavin. 'They think she was lying, and they keep sending her texts about her "imaginary boyfriend".'

'That's rotten,' said Alice.

'Totally,' said Gavin. 'So anyway, now that Robyn and I are ... friends, she's asked me to go to the party with her – for moral support.'

'That's sweet,' said Alice. 'I presume you said you'd go?'

Gavin nodded. 'Of course. I want to help her.'

'That's nice of you,' I said, thinking that the mean cousins couldn't pick on her if she showed up with a totally cool, nice boy like Gavin.

He smiled at me. 'Thanks, Megan,' he said. 'It's all sorted, but I just wanted to tell Mum and Dad before I go. The cousins live kind of far away, so we have to leave soon. And the party will go on very late, so we're going to stay in her aunt's house for the night.'

'Totally romantic,' said Grace, quickly ducking as he pretended to hit her.

'You and Robyn can have a beautiful day tomorrow,' said Alice. 'You could shake off the mean cousins and explore the other side of the island together.'

Gavin gave a dreamy smile. 'That would be nice, but it's not going to happen. Robyn's dad is dropping me back here first thing in the morning. He and Robyn are playing golf at ten.'

Grace checked her watch again. 'Mum and Dad should definitely be back by now,' she said. 'And it's totally weird that they haven't rung us.' For the first time, she was starting to look worried.

Gavin jumped up. 'You're right, Grace,' he said. 'They never stay away this long without letting us know where they are. I'm going to take a walk down to the security office. Maybe José has seen them.'

Just as he got to the door though, the phone in the kitchen rang.

'It's Mum,' he said, as he stood in the doorway and answered it. 'Hey Mum, what's up? Why aren't you ...?'

Then he stopped talking, and looked serious.

The rest of us didn't even pretend not to listen. 'He what? Oh, no. Is he OK? Poor Dad.'

He talked for ages, and the rest of us did our best to understand what was going on – not easy when we could only hear half of the conversation.

Finally he hung up. 'Dad fell when he was playing tennis this morning,' he said. 'José drove him and Mum to the hospital. They've just seen the doctor and she said that Dad's shoulder was dislocated.'

'Ouch,' said Alice. 'I don't like the sound of that.'

'So what happens next,' asked Grace. 'Can they relocate it?'

Gavin nodded. 'I'm not sure that's what they call it, but, yes, they're going to put it back into place soon. Mum says Dad will be fine once it's done, and that they should be home in a few hours.'

He looked at his watch again. 'Maybe I should stay here till Mum and Dad get back.

Maybe I should tell Robyn that I can't go with her to her cousins' place.'

'No way!' said Alice quickly. 'I mean, that probably isn't a good idea.'

'She's right,' said Grace. 'Poor Robyn – you promised her you'd go and you can't let her down. You can't leave her to face her mean cousins all on her own. You go ahead to the party. We'll tell Mum and Dad where you are.'

'I'm not sure,' he said, looking worried. 'Will you three be OK here until Mum and Dad get back?'

Grace rolled her eyes. 'We're *thirteen,*' she said.

'We're very sensible,' I said, meaning *Grace and I are very sensible and we'll keep an eye on Alice.*

'Well, maybe it would be OK,' said Gavin.'

'Of course it will be OK,' said Alice.

She jumped up and practically pushed him towards the stairs. 'Robyn will be waiting,' she said. 'So hurry up and get what you need. Remember you've got to impress the mean cousins, so you've got to look your best. I think you should bring your pale blue shirt – that's really cool, and your navy trousers and you should wear that aftershave that smells like lemons and ......'

Gavin laughed as he backed towards the stairs. 'I get it,' he said. 'I'm going.'

I didn't say anything. I thought I was the only one who'd noticed Gavin's lemon-scented aftershave.

Chapter Thirteen

After Gavin left to meet Robyn, the rest of us realised that we were hungry. 'I'll make lunch,' said Alice. 'I need to practise all the things I learned in home ec.'

Grace and I looked at each other and tried not to laugh. Alice isn't exactly the star of our home ec class. She'd been studying the subject for six months but she'd never once managed to produce anything you'd actually eat – unless you had a gun pointed at your head. Once she even managed to set off the smoke alarms and the whole school had to be evacuated. My best friend was always optimistic though – and she had a very short memory.

'You two relax in the sunshine,' she said. 'And I'll prepare a feast that you'll never forget.'

I totally didn't like the sound of that. I didn't want to hurt her feelings, though, so I bit my tongue and lay back on my sunlounger and tried to concentrate on my book.

Twenty minutes later, after lots of banging and crashing sounds, and a few rude words, Alice appeared with a huge tray.

'Ta-da!' she said. 'Lunch is served. I've made sandwiches.'

I began to relax a bit. After all, how much of a mess could you make of sandwiches?

Had Alice managed to be sensible for once in her life?

'Thanks, Alice,' I said. 'That's really nice of you. I'm starving.'

'There's three kinds,' she said proudly, as she put the tray down on a small table at the side of the pool.

'Yay,' said Grace as she sat up. 'What are they?

Mum and Dad haven't been shopping since the day before yesterday, so it must have been hard to find three different fillings.'

'All you need is a bit of imagination,' said Alice. 'And I've always had a good imagination.'

Suddenly I felt nervous. Sometimes Alice can be *too* imaginative.

'So tell us,' I said. 'What's in the sandwiches?'

'It was supposed to be a surprise,' said Alice with a big sigh. 'But since you're being so impatient, I'll tell you. But I'm warning you, you're going to be blown away.'

Now I felt even more nervous. 'Just tell us,' I said.

She smiled. 'You can choose between – 1. peanut butter, honey and red onions – 2. chocolate spread, cucumber and mayonnaise, or 3. cheese, banana and curry paste. Make up your minds, girls, which one do you want to try first?'

If I didn't know Alice better, I'd have thought

she was joking. I looked at Grace and she looked at me, and then we both looked at the sandwiches. They were cut into nice neat triangles, and looked harmless enough. Now that I knew what was in them though, I was afraid. I was very afraid.

'I know. I know,' said Alice. 'It's hard to decide. Here, I'll make it easy for you.'

She took two plates from the tray, and put one of each kind of sandwich onto each plate. Then she held the plates toward us.

Grace nodded at me and we both leaned forwards. We were in this together. We had to be strong for each other. We took the plates and rested them on our knees.

I sat looking at my sandwiches, wondering how I'd find the nerve to take the first bite.

'Hey, what's wrong?' asked Alice, when she noticed that no one was eating.

Before I could think of an answer, she jumped to her feet. 'Silly me,' she said. 'I forgot to bring out the ketchup. I'll be back in one second.'

When Alice came back, Grace's plate was empty and she was wiping her mouth. 'No need for ketchup,' she said. 'The sandwiches were totally delicious without it.'

Alice turned to me. 'Yum,' I said, holding up my empty plate, not able to look her in the eye.

Alice held the tray of sandwiches towards us again. 'Who's for seconds?' she asked. 'I've made plenty.'

Grace and I shook our heads enthusiastically. 'Totally full,' I said.

'Couldn't take another bite,' said Grace.

Then we watched with our mouths open as Alice quickly ate two of each kind of sandwich.

'Hey,' she said, when she was finished. 'You're right. These are totally delicious. I think there should be a law against boring sandwich fillings like cheese and ham and tomato. I think when I'm older I'm going to set up my own business. I can see it already. I could have plates and serviettes with a really cool logo saying

Alice's Suberb Sandwiches – or A.S. ... OK, so maybe that exact name wouldn't work. But I'll think of something. First though, I must remember to write down what ingredients I used today. These sandwiches could be the key to my future.'

She stopped talking when she noticed that Grace and I were nearly falling off our sun-loungers, we were laughing so much.

'Hey, what's so funny?' she asked.

Grace and I couldn't answer, and Alice's face went serious. 'You think I'm being a bit too ambitious, don't you?'

Still we couldn't say anything.

'Maybe I did get a small bit carried away,' said Alice. 'I guess it's a long way from one tray of sandwiches to a chain of successful restaurants.'

She looked so disappointed, I felt sorry for her.

'No,' I said. 'You go for it, Al. You go ahead and set up your sandwich company and I bet you'll make millions.'

'Thanks, Meg,' said Alice, smiling again. 'Thanks for believing in me. You're a true friend. I'm going to put a swimming pool in my first house, and you can come over and use it any time you like.'

And Alice lay on her sunlounger and closed her eyes and Grace and I looked at each other and shook our heads. Our friend was nice, but totally weird.

★ ★ ★

At six o'clock that evening the phone in the kitchen rang again and we all ran inside..

'Hey Mum,' said Grace when she picked up the phone. 'How's Dad? Have they relocated his shoulder? Did it hurt? When will you be home? You're probably tired after hanging around the hospital for so long, so Megan said she'll cook dinner for us all if you like. She's a really good cook, so you don't have to worry about us getting poisoned or anything and ...'

She stopped talking. 'Oh dear,' she said. 'Poor Dad. That sounds rotten. What? The whole night? So when will you be back? Oh. OK. Er no … he's … he's … in the shower. I'll tell him what you said though. Yeah, OK. Talk later. Bye. Give Dad a kiss for me.'

When she hung up, she didn't look happy. 'Poor Dad,' she said. 'They had to give him a pain-killing injection, and he's terrified of needles, and he fainted, and he hit his head on a trolley, and there was a big fuss, and they're afraid he might have concussion, so the doctor says he has to stay in hospital for the night.'

'Ouch,' said Alice.

'And what about your mum?' I asked.

'She says Dad's in a lot of pain,' said Grace. 'And hospitals and doctors scare him, and his Spanish is kind of rubbish, and Mum's is really good, so …'

'So what?' I asked. I wasn't sure I liked where this was going.

'So Mum's going to spend the night in the

hospital with Dad,' said Grace.

'Oh,' said Alice.

'But what about us?' I said. 'What are we supposed to do?'

'I'm not really sure,' said Grace. 'I didn't tell Mum that Gavin's gone away with Robyn for the night. If I did that, she'd have to come back here, and poor Dad would be all on his own. And if I phone Gavin and tell him what's happened, he'll come back from the party, and poor Robyn's night will be ruined.'

'We're *so* not going to let that happen,' said Alice. 'As long as your mum doesn't figure out that Gavin isn't here, everything will be fine.'

'But Mum said she'll ring again in a bit, and she'll want to talk to Gavin,' said Grace.

'Not a problem,' said Alice. 'We'll just make up an excuse, and say he's gone out for a few minutes. She'll never guess that he's gone away for the whole night.'

'But what if your mum rings Gavin's mobile?' I asked. 'She'll tell him about your dad, and he'll tell her that he's at the other side of the island. And then one of them will end up coming home.'

Part of me kind of hoped that one of them would come home. A few hours of minding ourselves was fine, but I didn't like the sound of a whole night without grown-ups.

What if burglars came?

Or there was a fire?

Or if one of us fell and broke her leg?

Grace shook her head. 'Mum can't call Gav. Her phone battery is dead, and Dad's phone is here, so she has to use a hospital phone.'

'But couldn't she use the hospital landline to call Gavin's phone?' I asked, trying not to sound too hopeful.

Grace shook her head again. 'Mum never knows anyone's mobile numbers, so even if she wants to call Gavin, she won't be able to. Any time she wants to talk to us, she's going to have to use the landline. As long as we don't say anything stupid, we're on our own for the night.

How cool is that?'

I still didn't like the idea. 'What about tomorrow?' I asked. 'What's going to happen when Grace's parents find out that we stayed here on our own? Won't we be in the biggest trouble ever?'

Alice grinned. 'I think we could get away with it,' she said. 'Gavin said he's going to get back early, so all we have to do is get up before he arrives, and mess up the kitchen a bit, so it looks like your mum spent the night here, and had breakfast here.'

'But she won't *be* here,' I said.

Alice rolled her eyes, like I was deliberately missing her point. 'So we just say she went back to the hospital to see Eddie.'

'And when Mum and Dad and Gavin all get together, won't they figure out what really happened?' asked Grace.

'Nah,' said Alice. 'Your dad will just talk about his shoulder, your mum will be worrying about packing to go home, and Gavin will be in a total dream after his romantic night with Robyn. They'll never join up the dots.'

'I think you could be right,' said Grace, smiling. 'I think we might actually get away with this.'

'Of course we're going to get away with it,' said Alice. 'Now stop worrying, Megan, and relax. We're home alone for a whole night. It's every kid's dream.'

I didn't say anything. Grace and Alice were all happy and excited, so how could I tell them that I was totally, totally scared?

Chapter Fourteen

Before long, it started to get cold. We folded up the towels, and straightened up the sunloungers and went inside to have our showers.

Grace and Alice had gone downstairs and I was sitting on my bed brushing my hair when Mum rang my mobile.

She did her usual routine of checking to see if I'd broken any of her rules about healthy eating and being careful in the sun and staying away from all kinds of imaginary dangers that only she could dream up. I couldn't concentrate properly on my answers though.

My mum has this secret radar that goes into overdrive when there's a problem.

What would she say if she knew what was really going on?

What would she say if she discovered that Alice, Grace and I were home alone?

Her last question was the worst one of all.

'It's been lovely talking to you, darling,' she said. 'Now, will you put me on to Grace's mum for a minute?'

'What do you want to talk to her for?' I asked.

'Oh, I just wanted to thank her for giving you such a wonderful time,' said Mum.

'Mum!' I said, trying to sound grown up. 'You'll only embarrass her. You've thanked her twenty times already, and I think that's probably enough. If you talk to her again she'll think you're stalking her and she'll want to call the police.'

And amazingly, Mum listened to me. 'Oh, very well,' she said. 'You're probably right. You just make sure she knows how grateful we are, OK?'

'Sure I will,' I said. 'Leave it to me. I'll thank her a hundred times before I go to bed. Now I'd better go, I think someone is calling me for dinner. Love you, Mum, bye.'

'I love you too,' she said. 'And so do Dad and Rosie and Domino. We're all looking forward to seeing you the day after tomorrow.' And then she hung up.

I listened to the beeping of the phone, and felt tears come to my eyes. Grace and Alice were downstairs planning all kinds of treats, but I couldn't help feeling nervous and afraid.

Then I shook my head, and sat up straight.

Megan Sheehan I said to myself. *You're not a baby any more. You're thirteen years old. It's time to grow up and stop being such a scaredy cat. It's time to have fun.*

Then I stood up and marched downstairs, trying very hard to look confident and happy.

★ ★ ★

I made a really nice pasta dish with cheese and cream and tomatoes. I even let Alice help – after she promised to do *exactly* what I told her.

While Alice and I were cooking, Grace took out all the best dishes and cutlery, and decorated the table with flowers. She filled a jug with lemonade and ice and fruit, and put on some really cool music.

The meal was fun. We pretended we were college students, having a dinner-party in our flat.

'Let's all live together when we're older,' said Alice. 'And every single night can be like this one. Every single night can be amazing.'

That did sound kind of cool, so I smiled as I served up the last of the pasta, and Grace poured us all more lemonade, and Alice turned the music up louder, and everything was perfect.

★　★　★

Gavin rang just as we finished eating, and Grace told him the story we'd agreed on.

'Oh, Dad's fine,' she said, rushing the words a bit. 'He'll be as good as new in a few days. He has to stay in hospital for the night though. No, you don't need to come back – Mum said it's not a big deal. The doctors are just being super-cautious. No, sorry, you can't talk to her. She's gone to bed and she said not to disturb her. She's kind of tired after sitting around the hospital for half the day. Yeah, I told her you're spending the evening in Robyn's cousin's place, and she's fine with that. She said it was kind of you to help her out. We'll see you tomorrow. I'll tell Mum you rang. Yeah, OK, bye.'

A second after she hung up, the phone rang again. 'Oh hi, Mum,' she said, a bit breathlessly. 'How is Dad feeling now? Oh, good. Tell him I love him. Yeah, we're all fine here. Alice made an ... interesting lunch and Megan made us a lovely pasta dinner.'

Then she hesitated and I knew she'd got to the hard bit. 'Oh, sorry, Mum, Gavin's asleep. He went for an extra-long run this afternoon, and he was wrecked after it, so he went to bed as soon as he'd eaten. He said to say goodnight to you. Yeah, we'll all be fine, don't worry about us. Yes, I'll lock all the doors and I'll put out all the lights when we're going to bed. We'll see you tomorrow, OK? Yes, love you too. Kiss Dad goodnight for me. Bye.'

When she hung up, Alice hugged her. 'Well done,' she said. 'That was perfect.'

'I feel bad though,' said Grace. 'I don't like telling lies – especially to my family.'

'Don't feel bad,' said Alice. 'Remember, we're doing a good thing here. Your mum is getting to stay with your dad while he's not well, and Gavin is making sure that Robyn doesn't get a hard time from her mean cousins. And we three will be fine here.'

'I guess you're right,' said Grace.

'Of course I'm right,' said Alice. 'It's all good. We're three responsible kids and everything's going to be fine.'

★ ★ ★

The three of us helped to tidy up after the dinner and then we threw ourselves on the couches in the living room and ate ice-cream and chatted and laughed. I felt all grown-up, like someone from a movie or a cool TV show.

'I've got a great idea,' said Alice after a while. 'Let's play the secrets game.'

I hate that game. (There's a reason they're called secrets.) I didn't say this though. Once Alice has made up her mind about something, it's pretty impossible to make her change it.

'You start then, Alice,' I said. 'You tell the first secret.'

I was trying to buy time so I could think of a secret I didn't mind sharing.

'OK,' said Alice. 'Let me think ... Oh, I know,

I have a great one. Years and years ago, I used to love playing with Mum's make-up. One day I sneaked into her bedroom to play with her new lipstick. She'd only got it the day before, and I knew it was really, really expensive. I'd just wound it up as far as it would go when I heard her coming up the stairs.'

'What did you do?' I asked. I felt scared even thinking about it. Veronica totally hates when anyone messes with her stuff.

'I didn't have time to think,' said Alice. 'I put the lid back on really quickly, but I hadn't wound the lipstick down, and it got all squished up and wrecked.'

'OMG,' I said.

'What happened?' asked Grace. 'Did your mum go crazy?'

'I haven't told you the worst part yet,' said Alice. 'I've never told anyone this before. I shoved the squished-up lipstick into my pocket, and later I put it under Jamie's bed. When Mum found it the next day, she blamed him.'

'That's awful,' I said. 'But didn't Jamie tell her that it was nothing to do with him?'

Alice shook her head. 'He was so small he couldn't talk properly. He could only say words like duck, and teddy and stuff, so he wasn't able to explain that he'd never touched the broken lipstick.'

'The poor kid,' said Grace. 'How could you do that to him?'

'Actually, it wasn't as bad as it sounds,' said Alice. 'Jamie was so small and cute, Mum didn't really get cross with him, even though she'd have *killed* me. Anyway, I survived, and that's the end of my secret. What's yours, Grace?'

Grace thought for a long time. 'I don't know,' she said in the end. 'I can't think of anything. I've told you two all my secrets already.'

'But you've got to think of something,' said Alice. 'That's the game.'

'OK' said Grace in the end. 'Since you insist – but you might be sorry, Alice, because my secret is to do with you.'

'What is it?' asked Alice leaning forward and looking excited. 'Will I be happy when I hear it?'

'Er ... I don't think so,' said Grace. 'My secret is that, at lunchtime, when you went inside to get the ketchup, I didn't eat any of the sandwiches you put on my plate.'

'So what did you do with them?' asked Alice. 'Were you saving them for later?'

'No,' said Grace quickly. 'I threw them over the hedge.'

That wasn't news to me, because I'd done exactly the same thing. I didn't want to hurt Alice's feelings, but there was no way I was going to eat those gross sandwiches.

'That's rotten,' said Alice. 'After all my trouble! Don't you feel guilty about wasting the food I prepared for you?'

'Not really,' said Grace giggling. 'My only worry is that maybe I poisoned the local wildlife. Sorry, Alice, but those sandwiches were just weird. I never would have told you, but you're the one who insisted on this stupid game.'

Alice turned to me, and I could see that she was really mad. 'What about you, Meg?' she asked. 'Did you throw my sandwiches away too?'

'If I tell you, does that count as my secret?' I asked.

'No!' said Alice crossly.

'Well then,' I said, avoiding her question, 'My secret is ...'

My biggest secret was that I thought Gavin was kind of cool, but there was nooooo way I was telling Grace and Alice that. They'd tease me in front of him, and it would be totally, totally embarrassing.

'Get on with it, Megan,' said Grace. 'What's your big secret?'

'OK,' I said slowly. 'My secret is – and I know it's kind of stupid – I was really afraid about staying here tonight without your parents, Grace. I didn't like the idea of being home alone.'

Alice leaned over to me. 'I already figured that out,' she whispered. 'So it's not exactly a secret.'

But she squeezed my hand, and I knew she wasn't going to give me a hard time.

'OK,' she said then. 'It's my turn again. Last year, when I was staying at my dad's place—'

I soooo didn't want any more of this game. I picked up a cushion, and whacked Alice on the head with it, and as soon as she had recovered she did the same to me. A second later, Grace joined in and we had a long cushion fight, that only ended when Alice collapsed on the couch and begged for mercy.

It was totally cool.

Chapter Fifteen

After the cushion fight we watched a DVD, and chatted some more. I was really tired, but it seemed a bit weird to go to bed when there wasn't an adult around to tell me I had to. So I rubbed my eyes, and tried to keep up with what Grace and Alice were saying.

In the end, when I thought I'd have to find some matchsticks to hold my eyes open, Alice gave a huge yawn.

'Bedtime?' she suggested, and no one argued.

We checked that all the doors and windows were securely locked. (And when the others weren't looking, I checked a second time, just to be sure to be sure.) Then we went upstairs and got ready for bed.

I was just pulling back my bedcovers, and getting ready to dive in, when Alice opened the balcony door.

'The sea is beautiful tonight,' she said as she looked out. 'Come and look, you two.'

Grace and I went and stood beside her. Alice was right. The navy-blue sky was full of twinkly stars, and the moon was shining on the distant sea, lighting up a silvery pathway, like something out of a fairytale.

'The three of us are so coming back here on our own when we're older,' said Grace. 'We'd have an amazing holiday.'

'That would be so cool,' said Alice. 'We should make a pact, and promise that we're going to do it, no matter what.'

'Hey,' I said. 'Why don't we take a photograph of the three of us here on the balcony? Our grown-up selves can look back, and see how totally cute we were when we were teenagers?'

'We should take a picture in the same place every time we visit,' said Alice. 'We can watch ourselves growing up.'

'That's a brilliant idea,' said Grace. 'I'll go get my camera.'

So Grace got her camera from the bedroom, and she spent ages figuring out how to work the self-timer, and then she had to balance the camera on the patio table, and it kept falling over, so Alice brought out the blanket from her bed to support it, and then the three of us lined up at the edge of the balcony, and put our arms around each other and said 'LANZAROTE!' all together really loud and the camera flashed and we all laughed and then there was a sudden gust of wind and the door into the bedroom slammed shut and Grace stopped laughing and said in a very quiet voice. 'Oh.'

'What?' I asked, noticing how worried she looked. 'What's wrong?'

'Now we are in very, very big trouble,' she

said. 'That's what's wrong.'

Alice ran over to the door. 'This is stupid,' she said. 'There's no handle on the outside. How are we supposed to open the door? How are we supposed to get back inside?'

'We can't,' said Grace. 'That door can only be opened from the inside. Gavin and his friend got stuck out here last year. They shouted for ages and it was nearly an hour before we heard them and set them free.'

'But there's no one to hear us shout,' I said in a quiet voice. 'We're all alone.'

'We can phone for help,' said Alice in a bright voice. 'Who's got their phone?'

Grace and I both shook our heads. 'Not me,' we said together.

'We're teenagers,' sighed Alice. 'Isn't there a rule saying that we should never be more than a few metres away from our phones?'

I looked through the glass to where our three phones were lined up on the lockers next to our beds.

'We *are* only a few metres away from our phones,' said Grace. 'Only trouble is, there's a locked door between them and us. They might as well be a million miles away.'

Alice leaned over the balcony and looked down. 'Maybe I could climb ...'

'No way,' I said, pulling her back. 'Don't even think about it. We're on the second floor remember? Things are bad enough, but I think they might be a bit worse if Grace and I were stuck up here, looking at you lying on the patio with a broken leg. Have you forgotten what happened when you climbed up that tree to rescue Domino?'

'You're right, Meg,' said Alice. 'That was a stupid idea. Maybe we could try shouting for help instead.'

'We'd be wasting our voices,' said Grace. 'Mum and Dad especially chose this villa because it was so private. We never hear a single sound from the other villas, and that means they won't be able to hear us either. Everyone's too far away.'

'But that means ...' began Alice.

'... that we have to wait until either Gavin or my parents come back to rescue us ...' said Grace.

'... that also means we're going to be on this balcony for the whole night,' I said, and I started to cry.

Chapter Sixteen

Alice and Grace hugged me until I stopped crying. That took a long time, and when they finally pulled away, I realised that I was very cold. I was in my bare feet, and I was wearing thin summer pyjamas. I couldn't help thinking of my lovely warm fleecy onesie, which was folded up on my bed at home. I shivered.

Alice picked up the blanket from the table, and wrapped it around me.

'There,' she said. 'That better?'

'Thanks, Al,' I said. I was afraid if I said any more, I was going to burst into tears again.

I sat on the swinging couch and looked around. Even though the balcony was big, the only furniture was the swinging couch, and the small glass table.

Why couldn't there have been a huge comfy bed, piled high with soft blankets?

Or a wardrobe full of warm fleeces and hoodies?

Or a vending machine serving hot chocolate and packets of crisps?

Or a telephone for emergencies?

'This is all my fault,' said Alice. 'I was the one who came out here to look at the stupid sea.'

'But I was the one who suggested taking the picture,' I said.

'And I should have propped the door open,' said Grace. 'I knew it couldn't be opened from the outside.'

'It doesn't matter whose fault it is anyway,' said Alice. 'We're stuck, and there's nothing we can do about it.'

As she said the last words, there was a sudden

gust of wind, and she shivered. She and Grace were both wearing light pyjamas like mine. Lucky Alice hadn't got around to taking her socks off, but, like me, Grace was barefoot.

'Hey,' I said. 'Come over here. No point in anyone freezing to death.'

Alice and Grace came over and sat beside me, and we wrapped the blanket around the three of us. For a minute, no one said anything. It would have been lovely sitting there, looking out at the beautiful sea, with my two friends beside me – if only the balcony door wasn't locked, and if Lorna and Eddie and Gavin were downstairs, and if, when we got tired all we had to do was go inside to our warm and cosy beds.

'We're going to be in soooo much trouble when Gav gets back,' said Grace. 'When he finds the whole house locked up, and Mum and Dad gone, and the three of us frozen nearly to death out here, he's going to figure out what happened.'

'Maybe he won't tell,' said Alice. 'He doesn't seem the sneaky type.'

'He's *not* the sneaky type,' said Grace. 'He's really cool most of the time – but he takes his role as big brother very seriously. He'll tell on us, I know he will. Mum and Dad are going to go crazy when they hear that we pretended to them that Gav was here, and pretended to Gav that they were here. I'm going to be grounded for days.'

'Lucky you,' I sighed. 'If my mum and dad find out about this, I'll be grounded for months – or maybe forever.'

'I don't care about being grounded,' said Alice. 'No one ever died from being grounded. I just hope we don't freeze, or starve to death. Or we could die of thirst. Anyone know how long a human can survive without water?'

Even though I was scared, I had to laugh. Trust Alice to be so dramatic.

'It's not going to go that far,' said Grace. 'Robyn and her dad are playing golf at ten, and they're dropping Gav back before their game. That means he should be here around nine. That's not so bad, is it? None of us will have starved to death by then.'

Unusually for her, Alice didn't say anything. I couldn't speak either. I huddled closer to my friends, and tried not to cry.

★ ★ ★

Usually, when Grace and Alice and I are together, we talk a lot. There never seems to be enough time to say all the things we want to say. Now though, when we had all the time in the world, we were silent.

I stared at the sky. Maybe if I saw a shooting star, it would be sign that everything was going to be OK. But I stared until my eyes were tired, and all the stars stayed in the same place, twinkling away madly, like they didn't care.

I thought about movies where groups of friends are trapped on a desert island, or in a cave high in the mountains. In those films, the friends always pass the time by saying deep, thoughtful stuff, like how much they love each other.

I couldn't think any deep thoughts though. All I could think about was how cold my toes were, and how hungry we were going to be if we couldn't get any breakfast, and what was going to happen when one of us wanted to go to the toilet.

This could get totally gross.

Chapter Seventeen

'About those secrets,' said Alice after a while.

'You can stop right now, Al,' I said. 'Things are bad enough already. There's no way I'm going to let you bully me into telling you more secret stuff.'

'Megan's right,' said Grace. 'That secrets game is stupid, and I'm not playing it any more.'

'It isn't a game this time,' said Alice. 'You two don't have to tell secrets if you don't want to.'

'We don't want to,' I said quickly. 'Game over.'

'But there's another secret I didn't tell you before,' said Alice. 'And I feel kind of bad about that.'

'So tell,' said Grace. 'It's not like Megan and I are going anywhere any time soon. We've got all the time in the world.'

'OK,' said Alice slowly. 'It's about Melissa.'

'Oh,' said Grace. (Grace used to be friends with Melissa, a long time ago, before she got sense.)

'What about Melissa?' I asked.

'The thing I want to tell you is that I met her last week,' said Alice.

'But that's not a secret,' I said. 'I was there with you, remember? Melissa tried to bully me as usual.'

'No,' said Alice. 'I don't mean that time. I met her again, the day after that.'

'And?' asked Grace. 'Why is that such a big deal? Melissa's always showing up. She comes home from boarding school every chance she gets.'

'We talked for ages,' said Alice. 'And Melissa was really upset '

'Oh, dear!' I said sarcastically. 'Was she sad

because I wasn't there for her to pick on? That must have been awful for the poor girl.'

'I'm being serious, Megan,' said Alice. 'Melissa was *really, really* upset. She's very unhappy at boarding school.'

'We knew that,' I said. 'She told us ages ago, remember. But what's all this about, Alice? It sounds like you care — except that's totally impossible. How could you care about some-one who's such a total bully?'

'Things have got worse since we last talked to her about her boarding school,' said Alice, ignoring my question. 'Melissa says she hasn't got a single friend there. She says she cries herself to sleep every night. She says she hates every minute she spends there.'

Normally, I'd have been sympathetic. I know what it's like to be sad and lonely. But it's hard to feel sorry for someone when their life's mis-sion is making *your* life a misery.

'So why doesn't she just change schools?' asked Grace. 'Wouldn't that fix things for her?'

'Melissa is afraid to tell her parents how unhappy she is,' said Alice. 'Her parents paid tons of money for that boarding school, and she doesn't want to disappoint them by telling them how much she hates it there.'

'That's kind of a problem,' said Grace.

'And there's more,' said Alice. 'Melissa's parents don't like our school very much. Her big sister made all these weird friends and went a bit crazy while she was there, so——'

'Whoa,' I said. 'Hold it right there. What are you saying? Do you mean Melissa wants to come to *our* school?'

'Of course,' said Alice. 'Where else would she go?'

A boarding school on Mars sounded good to me, but that was probably a bit cruel, so I didn't say it.

'I don't get why this whole thing about Melissa is a secret,' said Grace. 'Why didn't you tell us before?

'Well,' said Alice. 'I didn't say anything,

because I've been trying to work stuff out in my head. I've been thinking – maybe we should help Melissa.'

'How?' asked Grace.

'Well, we could go to her house and sort of casually meet her parents. We could talk about all the good stuff we do at our school, and how good it is for developing our personalities as well as our academic achievements.'

Grace giggled. 'You mean all that garbage the principal goes on about at assembly?'

'Yeah,' said Alice. 'That kind of stuff. And then Melissa's parents would realise that it wasn't the school's fault that her sister went crazy. And then ...'

'And then what?' I asked.

'And then, because we're there with her, Melissa will be brave enough to tell her parents how unhappy she is at boarding school, and they'll let her leave. I *know* it'll work. What do you think?'

Grace didn't answer. I sat there as all kinds of

emotions fought it out in my brain. I remembered what it was like when I was in sixth class, after Alice had moved to Dublin with her mum. Melissa picked on me nearly every day while Alice was gone. Every day she found something new to mock me for. Every morning I woke up feeling scared and lonely. Every morning I wanted to pull the covers up over my head, and hide from the world. I was always afraid of meeting Melissa – always afraid of the mean things she was going to say to me. It was the worst time of my life.

'So,' said Alice again. 'What do you think?'

Suddenly I realised I was really, really mad.

'I don't get you, Alice O'Rourke,' I said. 'I thought you were supposed to be my friend.'

'I *am* your friend,' she said.

'No, you're not,' I said as I wriggled free of the blanket and stood up to face her. 'You're totally not my friend. You know how Melissa hates me. You know how she picks on me every time we meet. If she comes to our school, I'll have to see her every single day.'

'Meg,' said Alice, reaching out to hold my hand.

I pulled away. 'No!' I said. 'Why would you want to help the girl I hate most in the whole world? Why would you want *me* to help her?'

'But—' said Alice.

I didn't let her finish. 'If Melissa comes back, she's going to ruin my life all over again,' I said. 'And this time it'll be totally your fault. Knowing my luck, she'll be put into my class, and you and Grace and Louise will be off having fun together, and I'll be just sitting there, waiting for Melissa to think up more mean stuff to say to me. I've got friends in my class now, friends who've never met Melissa, friends who actually think I'm kind of cool. As soon as Melissa shows up and starts saying mean stuff, they're all going to hate me. I might as well get the word "loser" tattooed on my forehead. Thanks a lot – best friend.'

I stopped as tears came to my eyes, making

Alice look all blurry and weird. I knew I'd been shouting, but I didn't care. I wanted to run inside, and throw myself on my bed and have a proper cry. But I couldn't do that. I was trapped and there was nowhere to run. Nowhere to hide.

I bit my tongue and tried to hold back the tears.

'Can I say something?' asked Grace.

Neither Alice nor I replied, so Grace spoke anyway.

'You both know I used to hang out with Melissa before,' she said. 'But we were never friends – not really. Mostly I was afraid of her.'

'I can see why,' I said. 'She's totally scary.'

'But then,' continued Grace. 'When I was in sixth class, I started to play hockey and I made lots of new friends. I started to feel more confident, and then I realised that I never should have been afraid of Melissa. I know she says bad stuff, and she picks on people—'

'Like me!' I said.

'But she's not tough, not really,' said Grace. 'Hidden underneath all her bullying is a really sad person. In the end, I mostly feel sorry for her.'

'What about feeling sorry for me?' I said angrily. 'I'm the victim here, remember? It's OK for you two to be all nice and forgiving, but I'm the one Melissa calls names and mocks and picks on.'

Alice got up and hugged me. I wanted to push her away, but something stopped me. Alice is a good hugger.

'Hey, Meg,' she said. 'I'm sorry you're so upset. I know Melissa has been mean to you. I know you used to be a bit afraid of her, but you're older now, and braver. You're smart and funny and you've got heaps of friends. You're ten times better than she could ever be.'

It was nice hearing my friend say such nice things, but I couldn't answer her.

'What could Melissa ever say that would really, really hurt you?' continued Alice.

'Lots,' I said. 'She's had years of practice. Once she called me a hippy loser in front of my mum, and Mum went on about it for weeks and weeks. Another time the teacher was reading a story about a crazy family, and Melissa said the family sounded exactly like mine, and everyone laughed – even the nice kids.'

Grace put her head down. 'I remember that day,' she said. 'I laughed. I'm really sorry, Megan. I just wanted Melissa to like me. I never stopped to think about how you must have felt. I really didn't stop to think at all.'

'That's OK, Grace,' I said. 'It was a long time ago. You've been really nice to me since then. Melissa hasn't changed though. She was mean to me in primary school, and she's still mean to me now. That's never going to change.'

'If she does come to our school, she probably won't try anything,' said Alice. 'But if she does, she won't get away with it. She'll have to deal with me and Grace and Louise and Kellie.'

I didn't answer.

Part of me wanted to forget all the mean things Melissa had done to me.

Part of me wanted to be the bigger person.

Part of me wanted to say — *yeah, Al, you're right. I'm being stupid. Melissa can't hurt me any more. She's unhappy, and we should try to help her.*

But how could I say that?

Just thinking about Melissa made me feel all tense and nervous inside. Thinking about Melissa made me feel like a scared little kid.

Alice slowly let me go. 'Just think about it for a while, Meg,' she said. 'I'd like to help Melissa, but if you don't want me to, then I won't. In the end, you can be the one who decides.'

'I need to think about that,' I said.

'Sure,' said Alice. 'Take your time. We've got all night.'

Then we sat down, and the three of us huddled together under our blanket and waited for the night to be over.

Chapter Eighteen

Along time passed. Without watches or phones, it was hard to tell if it was hours, or just very slow minutes. Sometimes Alice and Grace chatted a bit. I didn't say much though. I couldn't stop thinking about Melissa, and how horrible my life would be if she came to our school.

What if she got put into my class?

What if I had to look at her every minute of every day?

What if she made everyone hate me?

It would be like a nightmare – except that it would be true, and I'd never, ever get to wake up.

★ ★ ★

After a while, I fell asleep. I dreamed I was at home, playing with Rosie and Domino, and listening to Mum getting dinner ready in the kitchen. Then Dad came home and we all sat down to dinner, and even though the dinner was a big bowl of organic porridge, with no sugar on it, it was a nice dream.

When I woke up, it was still pitch dark. I was stiff and cold. My feet had poked out from under the blanket, and I felt like I had two blocks of ice strapped to the end of my legs. I tried to rub them back to life, but it wasn't easy, since my hands were cold too.

Beside me, Alice woke up. 'Hey, Meg,' she said. 'You OK?'

I shook my head sadly. 'No. Not really. I'm freezing. I thought this was supposed to be a warm country.'

Alice leaned down and a second later she pushed something into my hand.

'Here,' she said. 'Take these.'

'Your socks?' I whispered. 'But you need them.'

'I'm fine,' she whispered. 'I come from a long line of tough kids. Now put them on, while they're still warm.'

I didn't argue any more. I pulled the socks on, and wiggled my toes. Normally, I don't think a whole lot about socks, but now I felt like Alice had given me the best present ever.

'Thanks, Al,' I whispered.

'That's OK,' she whispered back. 'Any time.'

Then we cuddled together and slept some more.

★ ★ ★

When I woke up again, the sky was turning grey-blue. Next to me, Grace opened her eyes.

'It's morning,' she said. 'Sort of. How do you feel?'

'Hungry. Cold. Stiff. Bored.'

The two of us stood up. I tucked the blanket around Alice who was in a deep sleep, and walked over to the edge of the balcony. Below us, everything was quiet. I could see the trees waving gently in the breeze, and far away beyond them, the sea was grey and cold-looking.

'Why did your parents have to buy the biggest villa?' I moaned. 'The one that's miles away from everyone and everything?'

'It seemed like a good idea at the time.'

'I don't suppose you're expecting a cleaner, or a pool guy or anything to show up this morning?'

She shook her head. 'The cleaner won't come until after we leave tomorrow, and the pool man only comes every few days – and he was here yesterday. Sorry, Megan, but until Gavin shows up after his romantic date, it looks like this balcony is going to be our home.'

Just then, Alice woke up. 'Any news?' she asked hopefully.

'Not unless you're expecting something by carrier pigeon,' said Grace, as a seagull flew past, squawking loudly.

Alice sighed and pulled the blanket over her head. 'Wake me when it's all over,' she said.

I stood at the edge of the balcony for a long time. The sky turned bluer, and the sun came out. From inside the bedroom, we could hear the ping of a text arriving in Grace's phone.

'That's probably Gavin, texting to say that he's going to spend another night with Robyn and her mean cousins,' said Alice poking her head out from under her blanket. 'And soon we'll hear Lorna ringing the landline to say that Eddie has to spend another night in the hospital, and that she's going to stay with him, and they'll be so busy, they won't worry about us not replying, and we'll be stuck here for another day and a night. Maybe they'll all fly back home without us, and we'll die here, cold and alone.'

'Hey, Al,' I said as I went over to hug her. 'It's

not like you to be so negative.'

And then I remembered. 'You're hungry, aren't you?'

She nodded. Alice is always really cross when she's hungry.

'Maybe we could catch a seagull, and it could lay us an egg,' I said, trying to make her smile. It didn't work.

'Yum,' she said. 'A raw seagull's egg, that's just what I've been dreaming of all night.'

'Pancakes,' sighed Grace. 'I just might kill someone for a big plate of pancakes with bananas and chocolate spread. Or even one of your er ... creative sandwiches, Alice. I'd eat one of those now, if only I had the chance.'

I didn't think I was all *that* desperate. Then I remembered that I'd been dreaming of a bowl of my mum's organic porridge and I understood how hungry I was too.

After a bit, a small patch of sunshine spread across the corner of the balcony. Alice crawled out from under the blanket, and we dragged the couch over, so we could warm our legs.

'No sun cream, Megan?' said Alice. 'What would your mum say? Maybe you should move into the shade?'

I sighed, and stretched my legs out further into the sun. 'I'm going to risk it,' I said. 'And Mum might just forgive me for sunbathing without factor 1,000 on my skin – if it saves me from dying of the cold.'

Suddenly Grace jumped up. 'OMG,' she said. 'Look over there, on the beach path – beyond the trees. There's people walking.'

Alice and I jumped up too. 'We're saved' she said. 'We're saved. We're not going to starve to death on this balcony after all.'

She started to jump up and down and scream. 'Over here. We're over here. We're trapped on this balcony. Come and rescue us.'

'You might as well save your voice,' said Grace. 'They're too far away. They'll never hear us.'

'But we can't just let them get away,' I said.

'We have to do something.'

Alice turned around and picked up the blanket and started to wave it madly in the air. It would have been funny, if I hadn't so desperately wanted it to work. And then, amazingly, one of the people stopped walking.

'They've seen us,' I whispered. 'They've definitely seen us.'

The other people stopped walking too. They were really far away, so it was hard to tell for sure, but it looked like they were looking at us. Alice was going crazy. She was waving the blanket so wildly, I was afraid she was going to fly away.

I was starting to think how stupid we were going to sound when the rescuers got here.

And whether they'd be able to get a key from José, so we could finally get off the balcony.

And if they'd ask hard questions about why we were home alone.

And what I was going to have for breakfast.

And then I saw something terrible.

'They're waving at us,' said Grace. 'I can't believe they're just waving at us.'

'They think we're only being friendly,' said Alice.

She was right. Each of the faraway figures gave a few waves, and then they turned and continued to walk. A minute later, they were gone, hidden by the trees on the side of the path.

Alice, Grace and I sat on the couch again. For a minute we'd been hopeful, and now that that hope was gone, I felt even worse than I had before. I felt like one of the balloons at Jamie's party – all pathetic and deflated and sad.

'I wonder what time Gavin will get here,' said Alice.

'I wonder how mad Mum and Dad are going to be,' said Grace.

'Maybe they'll feel so sorry for us that they won't be mad at all,' I said.

'Yeah, you're right, Megan,' said Grace. 'They might feel sorry for us – in about a hundred years time, when they've finished being mad. I should never have lied to them. They're cool about lots of stuff but they hate lies. Lying is the one thing that drives them totally crazy.'

Alice leaned over and hugged her. 'The three of us were in on it,' she said. 'We'll all share the blame.'

'Of course we will,' I said.

'Thanks, guys,' said Grace. 'That's nice of you.' But I could see that our words hadn't made her feel any better.

The three of us sat there, like criminals waiting for a judge to arrive to tell us how long our prison sentence was going to be.

Chapter Nineteen

Alice heard it first. 'OMG,' said, jumping up. 'There's a car. There's a car. Someone is coming. It must be Robyn's dad dropping Gavin back.'

Grace and I jumped up and looked over the balcony. Alice was right. We couldn't see anything, but there was definitely the sound of a car engine – and it was getting closer.

I hardly dared to breathe as the sound of the engine became louder and louder.

Don't turn back I whispered to myself. *Please don't turn back.*

The engine slowed down and we could hear the sound of tyres on gravel. A second later, José's minibus came around the corner and stopped near the front door. He climbed out slowly, and stretched, showing gross damp patches under his arms. I was prepared to overlook his underarms though. I don't think I've ever in my life been so happy to see another human being.

'Hey, José,' called Grace. 'Up here. We're up here.'

He shielded his eyes against the sun as he looked up. 'Hola, Grace,' he said. 'I hope you are enjoying this lovely day. I came to ask ….'

'José, we're trapped on the balcony,' said Grace. 'And Gavin's …… not here. Can you come and open the door for us please?'

'Goodness me,' he said. 'You poor girls. Let me get the spare key.'

We watched as he leaned into the minibus, and pulled out a huge set of keys. He spent ages and ages trying to figure out which was the right one. When he finally found it, he unlocked the front door, and we could hear the sweet sound of his footsteps on the wooden stairs. A second later, we saw him walking slowly across the bedroom, like there was no need to rush at all. When he finally opened the balcony door, I raced past him and into the toilet.

When I came out, Grace ran in, almost knocking me down in her hurry.

José laughed. 'Dear me,' he said. 'You are making me think you girls have been out there all night.'

Alice gave a big fake laugh. 'Ha, ha,' she said. 'That's really funny, José. Did you hear that, Megan? He thinks we've been on the balcony all night.'

'Ha, ha,' I said. I didn't think I was being very convincing, but luckily José laughed too.

'I am glad you like my joke,' he said. 'That makes me happy.'

When Grace came out of the bathroom,

José was examining the balcony door. 'I have spoken to your father about this lock many times,' he said. 'He has to get it fixed. One day, I am telling you, someone will get stuck out here for a very long time, and that will not be funny – not funny at all.'

'You're so right, José,' said Alice. 'That totally wouldn't be funny.'

'I think we'll go downstairs now, José,' said Grace. 'We haven't had our breakfast yet.'

'Dear me,' said José, laughing. 'Young people these days, always hungry.'

Grace, Alice and I raced downstairs, leaving José looking at the balcony door.

After I'd had a few spoons of cereal, I started to feel a bit better. I sat at the kitchen counter, feeling free and happy. After a while, Grace looked at her phone.

'That text you got earlier,' I asked. 'Was it from Gavin? Did he say anything about what time he's going to be back?'

She shook her head. 'It was just Kellie, telling me the latest news from pony camp. Gavin hasn't been in touch.'

'That's good, isn't it?' asked Alice.

'I think so,' said Grace.' But have you noticed? José hasn't asked any hard questions. He hasn't copped on that we spent the night here on our own. He probably thinks that Gavin's gone for a run or something. We might just get away with this. We might ...'

She stopped talking as José came into the kitchen.

'The reason I came is to ask how your poor father is,' he said. 'That was a very nasty fall he had yesterday. Your mother called me last night, and said they were staying in hospital for the night. Since she is not answering her mobile phone, I decided to come up here and see if you had heard from them. I thought maybe they might need me to pick them up. I thought ...'

He didn't finish, as the landline started to ring.

Grace picked it up. 'Oh, hi, Mum,' she said. 'Oh, great, that's really good news. Tell him I'm very happy he's allowed to come home. Oh, nothing much – same old, same old. Yes, we're all fine. Oh, José's here actually, will I put him on? OK, See you soon. Love you too. Bye.'

She handed the phone to José, and we could hear him arranging to go to the hospital to pick her parents up.

A few minutes later he drove away, and Alice, Grace and I went to lie by the pool, like nothing at all had happened.

★ ★ ★

Half an hour later, Gavin showed up. He looked tired, but happy.

'Good night?' asked Alice.

'Actually it was a really good night,' he said. 'It was nice to see how Spanish people celebrate. Robyn's cousins aren't that mean once you get to know them, and I think she had a good time too. I'm glad I went. Anyway, where's Mum, Grace? Is Dad home from hospital yet?'

I looked at Grace. Her face was red, and I knew she was thinking about telling him the truth.

Was this the moment when we were going to get into a whole lot of trouble?

But before Grace could answer, there was the sound of a horn beeping, and José's minibus appeared.

'Oh, there they are,' said Alice.

We all rushed over and watched as Eddie and Lorna climbed slowly out.

José waved at us from the driver's seat. 'Got to go. Busy, busy. Enjoy your last day!' he said, and then he drove away.

Eddie looked pale and tired, and his arm was in a sling, but otherwise, he didn't look too badly damaged.

Gavin got cold drinks for us all, and then everyone sat around the patio table, and I waited for the trouble to start.

Eddie told us all about his injury, and how it had to be fixed, and he made it all sound exciting and funny.

Lorna told us that when Eddie fainted, he'd knocked down a trolley full of sample bottles, and stuff went everywhere, and a nurse screamed at her while they all raced around picking up bottles of wee and blood and all kinds of gross stuff.

Then Gavin told us all about the party with Robyn's Spanish family and how crazy, but nice, they all were.

And Grace and Alice and I looked at each other and said nothing at all.

When we'd finished our drinks, the three of us went and sat by the pool.

'I can't believe it,' whispered Grace. 'Mum and Dad haven't copped on that Gavin spent the whole night with Robyn's family. They think he came back here after the party.'

'And Gavin hasn't copped on that your mum spent the night at the hospital,' said Alice. 'He must think that she stayed here, and then went with José this morning, when he was going to pick your dad up.'

'We've got away with it!' said Grace. 'We've totally got away with it. We didn't die of cold or thirst or hunger or anything, and we're not in trouble. Who ever saw that coming?'

I giggled nervously. 'Maybe one day, your parents will join up the dots, and figure out what happened, but let's hope that day is a very, very long time from now.'

'Yeah,' said Alice. 'I'm with you on that. When we're fifty, they can't really give us a hard time for spending a night home alone when we were thirteen, can they?'

'Too late to ground us then,' said Grace. 'Thirty-seven years too late.'

Just then, Lorna came over, and we stopped talking and looked at her innocently. 'You poor girls,' she said. 'You've nearly been forgotten about, with all the excitement of Eddie's accident, and Gavin's big night out with Robyn.

You probably wish you had some excitement in your lives too.'

I could feel my face going red, but Alice just laughed. 'Nah,' she said. 'We're good thanks, Lorna. Now pass me that sun-lotion Megan. We've only got a few hours left to work on our tans.'

★ ★ ★

That night, Robyn came over and Gavin cooked a big barbecue feast. Grace, Alice and I were tired after our long night on the balcony, so we headed up to bed early.

After carefully propping the door open with a huge heavy book, we stepped out on to the balcony. I looked out at the stars and the sea. I felt kind of sad, knowing that the next night I was going to be back home, with only my boring back garden and Mum's rows of cabbages and broccoli to look at.

Also, I felt kind of scared. I still hadn't told

Alice what I'd decided about the whole Melissa thing – mostly because I hadn't decided anything. I was trying not to think about it, but that wasn't working. Every few minutes, Melissa's mean, smiling face popped into my head, like she was haunting me.

'Hey,' said Alice, nudging me. 'Look down there.'

I looked where she was pointing, and saw Gavin and Robyn sitting on the side of the pool, dangling their legs in the water. They were holding hands and whispering and looking totally romantic.

'That's adorable,' I said.

'So sweet,' said Alice. 'And so sad. After all our hard work, it's awful to think that those two are going to be parted tomorrow.'

'Didn't you hear the news?' asked Grace. 'They're not going to be parted for long.'

'How come?' I asked.

'Robyn's going to be working here for the whole summer – she got a job in the kiddies' club. They only told her this afternoon.'

'And is Gavin going to come here for a holiday?' asked Alice.

'Better than that,' said Grace. 'He's applied for a job here as assistant lifeguard, and José says he's probably going to get it. That means that Gav and Robyn will be able to spend the whole summer together. How cool is that?'

'Totally cool,' said Alice.

I was so happy for them, I didn't say anything. Mum and Dad say I can't have a boyfriend until I'm sixteen, and that feels like it's a hundred years away. When the time comes though, I hope I meet a boy like Gavin.

That would be really, really nice.

Chapter Twenty

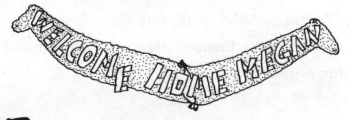

Eddie and Lorna dropped Alice off at her mum's place first. Grace and I got out of the car too, and the three of us hugged like we weren't going to see each other for a hundred years.

'See you both tomorrow?' said Alice when she finally pulled away.

'Sure,' said Grace, climbing back into the car. 'I'll call over for you.'

I hesitated for a second. I'd spent all of the flight home worrying and trying to make up my mind.

'About Melissa,' I said. 'I'm still not sure ...'

'Hey,' said Alice. 'Don't sweat it. We'll talk tomorrow, and remember, Megan, you're my friend, I won't do anything you don't want me to.'

'Thanks, Al,' I said, and then I gave her another quick hug and climbed back into the car.

★ ★ ★

'OMG,' said Grace. 'That's just ... OMG!'

I was busy cuddling Domino, and at first I couldn't see what she was talking about..

'OMG,' was all I could say when I looked up.

The front windows of our house were all decorated with tiny Spanish flags, and on the door was a huge banner saying – *WELCOME HOME, MEGAN.*

'I'm going to die,' I said. 'I'm going to totally die.'

Gavin smiled at me. 'I think that's a very sweet banner,' he said, making me feel a tiny, tiny bit better.

Grace leaned out of the window to get a

better look. 'It's cute,' she said. 'And isn't it good to know that your family missed you?'

'It is?' I asked. 'And why did they have to miss me so publicly?'

Before I could say anything else, the front door of my house was flung open and Mum came racing down the path. She was making a squeaky happy noise, and her heavy boots made her sound like a stampeding herd of elephants. Her hair was all messy, she was wearing an ancient, raggy apron. There was a big floury mark on her forehead. Domino wriggled out of my arms and ran and hid under a bush. I wished I could follow her.

Mum grabbed me and hugged me so hard I thought my ribs were going to break. Then she let me go and leaned into the car to shake Eddie and Lorna's hands.

'Thank you so much for bringing my baby back to me,' she said. 'I hope she was good and helpful and not too demanding. I hope she didn't make a nuisance of herself.'

'She was the perfect guest,' said Lorna. 'She's welcome to join us on holidays any time.'

'She didn't do a single thing wrong the whole time we were there, did you, Megan?' said Eddie.

'Er, no,' I said. 'Absolutely not. Thank you for everything. I had a lovely time.'

'Maybe you'd all like to come in for a cup of herbal tea?' said Mum then. 'I've made a special welcome home cake for Megan.'

Eddie hesitated. He loves cake – but then, in his world, cakes are made of nice stuff like chocolate and marshmallows.

'It's carrot and courgette cake,' said Mum with a big smile.

'Thanks, but no,' he said quickly. 'We need to go home to unpack.'

'The cake is sugar and fat-free,' said Mum.

'Well in that case, we *definitely* need to get home,' said Eddie, before Lorna dug him in the ribs with her elbow. Eddie groaned and started the car.

'Bye, everyone,' I said. 'And thanks again. See you tomorrow, Grace?'

'Great,' she said.

Eddie started the engine and Mum and I waved until they had driven around the corner at the end of our road.

Mum put her arm over my shoulder, and half-dragged me up the path, like I was going to vanish into thin air if she let me go. When we got to the front door, I could see that the welcome home banner was made of cut-up milk cartons and an old pair of tights.

'Isn't it lovely?' said Mum. 'I found the instructions on the internet, and Rosie and I spent a whole morning making it.'

Suddenly I felt cross. Why couldn't I have cool parents like Lorna and Eddie?

'Mum!' I said. 'That is totally embarrassing and OTT. You're forgetting that I was only in Lanzarote for a week. It's not like I've come back from a two-year expedition to the top of Mount Everest. Why do you have to make a big deal of everything?'

And then something terrible happened. Mum's face went all crumpled, like she was going to cry. 'We missed you, Megan,' she said. 'That's all. And we wanted to do something special to welcome you back. I thought you'd be happy.'

I felt really, really bad. 'Sorry, Mum,' I said. 'I'm just tired after the journey. The banner is lovely. It was nice of you and Rosie to make it for me.'

Mum smiled. 'Really?'

I smiled back at her. 'Absolutely,' I said.

As I let Mum lead me into the house, I wondered how soon I could take the banner down and hide it in the darkest corner of my bedroom.

Some things are too embarrassing for words.

Chapter Twenty-One

Two days later, I called over to Alice's place.

'Megan!' said Veronica when she opened the door. 'How are you? How is my favourite party planner?'

She lunged at me with a big hug, and I had to duck to avoid her sharp fingernails which came dangerously close to my eyes.

Before I could answer her question, she asked another one. 'Do you know I've been telling all my friends about you and how you saved Jamie's party? You could go into business, and make a fortune. You could do birthdays and confirmations and even weddings when you get a bit older. I can help you to draw up a business plan if you like.'

'Er, thanks, Veronica,' I said. 'I'll get back to you about that.'

I used to think that Veronica didn't like me, and that kind of scared me. Now she really, really liked me, and for some reason, that scared me even more.

Alice came into the hall and rescued me. I followed her into her room, and lay on her bed.

We listened to music for a bit, but we didn't talk much.

After a while she checked the time on her phone. 'It's nearly three o'clock,' she said. 'Melissa will be waiting. We should ......'

'I know,' I said, standing up. 'We should go.'

'It's not too late,' she said. 'You can still change your mind.'

We'd talked about if for hours and hours the

night before. In the end I'd agreed that the two of us were going to meet Grace at Melissa's place to put Alice's plan into action. Alice had even called Melissa and told her all about it. When we made the decision, it had seemed like a great idea. Now though, in the cold light of day, I wasn't so sure any more.

'*You* should still try to help Melissa,' I said. 'But maybe I shouldn't go with you. Maybe it's best if you and Grace go without me.'

'You're the one who will have to make that decision, Meg,' she said. 'I totally think you should come though. If you do this, you'll be the one taking control. You'll be showing Melissa that you're not afraid of her.'

'But I *am* afraid of her.'

She hugged me. 'That's not the point. Dad says that only fools never feel afraid. Brave people feel afraid, but they don't let that stop them from doing the right thing. You're brave, Megan – you always have been.'

I pulled away from her.

'I think I can do this,' I said.

She laughed. 'You can *totally* do this. Now let's go. Grace and Melissa will be waiting.'

As I walked along, part of me felt mature and strong and grown-up.

But in the back of my mind I could hear a mean, sneaky voice:

Once you do this, there will be no going back.

If this plan works, Melissa will be back in a big way.

What if you're making the biggest mistake of your whole life?

★ ★ ★

Melissa's house was huge, with a big gravel driveway, and two fancy shiny cars parked outside. Alice and I stood on the front doorstep, next to two giant-sized trees in pots.

'I feel like a little girl in a fairytale,' I whispered nervously. 'I feel like I've come to confront the wicked witch. I feel like, if I'm not careful, I'm going to get turned into a lizard or a stick insect or something.'

Alice giggled. 'Melissa's just a girl like you and me,' she said. 'Sometimes I think you forget that.'

She held her finger near the shiny brass doorbell.

'But I know you're scared,' she said. 'And I totally get why. Say the word, Megan, and we'll turn around and forget this whole thing. We can act like none of this happened – ever.'

'But Grace is on her way, and Melissa will be waiting. You promised her we'd be here. You promised we'd help her.'

'I know I promised,' said Alice. 'And I don't like breaking promises – but if I have to, I will. I can tell Melissa that we've changed our minds. I won't have to explain why. We can just walk away.'

'But ...'

'Don't you get it, Megan?' said Alice. 'I'm not going through with this unless you're absolutely sure about it. You're my very best friend in the whole world. I know that if I live until I'm five hundred, I couldn't possibly find another friend like you. I would never, ever do anything to hurt you.'

I smiled. With Alice as my friend, I could do anything I wanted.

'Go for it,' I said. 'I'm ready.'

Alice smiled at me too as she pressed the doorbell. A jangling sound echoed through the house. Then there was a moment's silence, followed by the click clack of footsteps.

The game was on.

★ ★ ★

Melissa opened the door and brought us inside. I'd never been in her house before. It was all shiny and bright and cold – a bit like a show house that no one had ever lived in. Melissa looked totally cool in a very fancy top and jeans, and her hair was all swishily shiny and perfect. She looked pale though, and worried.

'Let's not do anything yet,' she said. 'Let's just wait here until Grace shows up.'

That was fine with me. We could spend the whole day hanging out in her hall, if that's what she wanted.

Melissa kept fiddling with her fancy gold bracelet and looking nervously towards the back of the house. Knowing that she was scared made me feel a small bit better.

We stood in the hall for what felt like ages. I had lots of time to look at the fancy carpet on the stairs and the fancy stained-glass windows and the fancy chandelier with its cold, twinkly light.

Then the doorbell rang loudly and I jumped.

Melissa opened the door. 'It's Grace,' she said, like that was a big surprise.

The four of us stood in the hall. I felt embarrassed and scared and unhappy all at once.

'Maybe we could go to town or something,' said Melissa. 'I've got money, and I could treat

us all to hot chocolates and then we could go
to the cinema.'

That sounded good to me, but Alice shook
her head.

'Sure,' she said firmly. 'That sounds like a
really good plan, Melissa. I'd love to go to town
and drink hot chocolate and see a movie – but
not yet. First we've got a job to do, and I think
it's time we got started.'

'Er, I suppose you're right,' said Melissa.
'Mum and Dad are in the kitchen.'

Melissa led the way, walking slowly, like she
was going to a funeral or something.

She stopped at the kitchen door, which was
closed. She put one hand on the doorknob, but
she didn't turn it.

'I think we need to discuss this a bit more,'
she said, 'it's not good to rush into things.'

For once in my life, I found myself agreeing
with her.

'Melissa's right,' I said, trying not to choke
on the most unexpected words I'd ever said.

'Maybe we should.........'

Alice rolled her eyes. 'You guys!' she said. 'We've got a plan and we're sticking to it. Now step aside, Melissa, we're going in.'

Melissa stepped aside, and Alice turned the knob of the kitchen door and I tried to ignore the million butterflies that were battling it out in my stomach.

Chapter Twenty-Two

The kitchen was about the size of my whole house. Everything seemed to be made of metal or glass or shiny marble. It hurt my eyes a bit.

Melissa's mum and dad were sitting at opposite ends of the kitchen table, looking really busy typing stuff into their laptops.

'Hey, Mum and Dad,' said Melissa. 'These are my friends, Alice and Megan, and you know Grace already.'

'Hello, girls,' said both parents, without even looking up.

Then we all stood there for a bit, feeling totally awkward.

In the end, Grace pulled something from her pocket, and unfolded it. 'Here, Melissa,' she said. 'Here's the new brochure from our school – the one I was telling you about. Look, there's a picture of the new hockey pitch. It's got this super-modern surface – we're the first school in Munster to have one like it.'

'That's really cool,' said Melissa. 'Let's have a look.'

I wasn't paying much attention to the brochure, or to Melissa. I was watching her parents, who hadn't looked up from their work, not even for a single second. While Melissa studied the brochure, the only sound was the clicking of laptop keys.

Sometimes my mum drives me crazy, the way she wants to know every single detail about my life. When I bring friends over, she force-feeds them with healthy treats and asks totally inappropriate questions about their feelings.

Suddenly I felt that was a bit better than Melissa's parents, who didn't even seem to know that we were there.

I could see that Alice was getting edgy. She pulled the brochure from Melissa's hand and held it in front of her mum's laptop screen.

'Look,' she said. 'You should read this, so you can see all the great things about our school. There's a page on the drama society, and the music society, and here's a bit about a school trip to the science fair, and here's the home ec room – our teacher is brilliant, and home ec is my favourite subject, and I think I'm quite good at it, and here's …'

Melissa's mum finally looked up. She stared at Alice like she was a bit crazy.

Grace stepped forward. 'It's a great school,' she said. 'We came second in the hockey league last year, and our debating team is in the national finals next week.'

Alice was nudging me, and I knew I had to say something. Only trouble was, Grace and

Alice had already said all the things I'd planned to say. My mind was a blank, which is never really a good thing.

Everyone stopped talking, like they were waiting for me to say something very clever.

I looked desperately around the room, and saw a newspaper on a chair in the corner. Suddenly I had a flash of inspiration.

'Er ... I saw something amazing about our school in the newspaper last week,' I said.

'What was that?' asked Alice smiling at me like I was some kind of idiot.

'Er ... it said that one of our past pupils has just been made vice-president of the biggest computer firm in America. It's a brilliant job, and she was really lucky to get it.'

Now, for the first time, Melissa's dad looked up from his laptop. 'That's very interesting,' he said. 'Computers are the future. If you want to get on these days, a good grounding in computers is essential.'

'Vice-president?' said Melissa's mum. 'That's

very impressive. You can always tell a good school by where the graduates end up.'

Alice grinned at me, and I was starting to feel good, when her mother said, 'Now, Melissa, as you can see, Dad and I are rather busy, and we've wasted enough time with this chit-chat. Maybe you'd like to take your friends into the living room, and you can watch the DVD I bought you yesterday.'

'Great,' said Alice. 'I love watching DVDs, but first ......'

Melissa was madly shaking her head at Alice. I could see that she'd changed her mind about the plan. I could see that she was still too scared to tell her parents how unhappy she was at her boarding school.

Alice ignored her, though, and continued, 'I think Melissa has something she wants to say to you.'

Melissa looked like she was going to die, but Alice gave her a look that managed to be sym- pathetic and scary all at the same time. When she looks at me like that, I know there's no point in resisting.

'Mum, Dad,' said Melissa, in such a weird voice that both her parents looked up at the same time.

'I need to tell you something,' she said.

'What is it, darling?' said her mum, in a concerned voice, looking at her watch at the same time.

'I don't want to go back to boarding school for second year. I want to change to the local school, where Grace and Alice and Megan go.'

'But that boarding school is the best in the country,' said her mum.

'And you're so happy there,' said her dad.

'And you've made so many friends,' said her mum.

Now Melissa's voice was all choky. 'I'm *not* happy there,' she said. 'I've *never* been happy there.'

'But you said ...' began her mother.

'After you spent all that money on fees, I

didn't want to tell you the truth,' said Melissa. 'I didn't want to make you angry. So all this time I've been pretending. I haven't got any friends in boarding school – not a single one. I hate it there. I want to leave. Please let me leave.'

Now Melissa collapsed into loud sobs. Her skin went all red and blotchy and she didn't look perfect or confident or scary any more. She just looked sad and lost. I wondered how I'd ever been afraid of her.

'You poor baby,' said her mum.

'My little darling,' said her dad.

They both came over and hugged her for a long time. They patted her hair and stroked her back and whispered in her ear. It was a bit embarrassing, standing there watching them. I guessed they had forgotten we were there.

I looked at Alice and Grace. It was time for us to leave. As the three of us tip-toed towards the door, Melissa and her parents untangled themselves.

'I didn't realise that the local school was so

good.' Melissa's mum was saying. 'It must have improved after your sister left.'

'I didn't realise it either,' said her dad. 'Vice-president of a huge computer company, I have to say I *am* impressed. I'll phone the school tomorrow and see about enrolling you for September, Melissa. How does that sound?'

Melissa started to jump up and down, making these funny, giggly noises.

Alice, Grace and I didn't wait to hear Melissa's answer. Our job was done. We closed the door behind us, and left.

★　★　★

'You did it, Alice!' said Grace as we walked along. 'You really did. You're amazing.'

'It wasn't just me,' said Alice. 'You two did as much as I did.'

'But it was your idea,' I said. 'You're the one who wanted to help Melissa in the first place, and you're the one who came up with the plan.'

'I didn't think it was going to work at first,,' said Alice. 'I was beginning to think we were wasting our time. Melissa's parents didn't seem to care about the new hockey pitch, or the debating team or the music society.'

'Yeah,' said Grace. 'I thought it was turning into a total fail. I thought maybe we were making things worse for Melissa instead of better.'

'You're the one who made it work in the end, Meg,' said Alice. 'It's so lucky you'd seen that thing about the super-computer woman in the newspaper.'

I didn't answer.

'Meg?' said Alice. 'Did you hear what I said? Don't you think it's totally lucky that ......?'

Alice stopped walking and stared at me. Sometimes she has this funny way of looking at me, like my thoughts are on the outside, just waiting for her to notice them.

'No way,' she said.

I smiled.

'OMG!' said Alice. 'Just OMG!'

'What?' asked Grace.

'Megan made up the whole thing about the computer vice president. You're a genius, Meg. You really are.'

'Thanks,' I said sweetly.

'How did you think of it?' asked Alice.

'Well I was desperate,' I said. 'You and Grace were saying all this amazing stuff, and none of it was working. Melissa's parents were barely listening to a word you said. And then you nudged me to say something, and all I could see was the newspaper and their two laptops, and suddenly I realised that the only way to their hearts was through their computers.'

'That was clever,' said Grace. 'But won't Melissa's parents find out that you made the whole thing up? And what's going to happen then?'

Alice grinned. 'Hopefully, by the time Melissa's parents discover the truth, it'll be too late. Melissa will have got what she wanted. She'll be in our school.'

'Oh,' I said, suddenly remembering what we'd just done. 'Melissa is going to be in our school.'

Chapter Twenty-Three

We decided to hang out in Grace's place for a while.

'Is Gavin home?' I asked, trying not to sound too interested. I wanted to tell him that I'd already been to the swimming pool to practise the strokes he'd helped me with.

Grace nodded. 'I think he's home – and he's totally happy. José rang this morning to tell him that he's definitely got the lifeguard job.'

'That's fantastic news,' I said, as we followed her upstairs.

'Yeah,' said Grace. 'It is. And he spent about an hour on Skype to Robyn, planning the amazing summer they're going to have together.'

'Totally sweet,' said Alice. 'Happy ever after,

and it's all down to us.'

★ ★ ★

'There's one weird thing about Melissa's family that I forgot to tell you,' said Grace when the three of us were lying on her bed.

'What?' I asked, not sure I wanted to hear the answer.

She sat up. 'Well, can you remember why Melissa's parents didn't like our school?'

'Yeah,' said Alice. 'The biggest reason was that her sister went a bit crazy while she was there, and she started to hang out with all these weirdoes.'

'Only thing is,' said Grace. 'Melissa's sister and her friends are really nice. They're not crazy at all.'

'Are you sure?' I asked, remembering the girl I'd met once. She had black lipstick and spiky hair and about five nose-piercings. One Saturday I'd seen her coming towards me with a big gang of girls all dressed in black, and I was so scared I ran into a shop to hide.

'Suzie *looks* a bit crazy,' said Grace. 'But that's just an image. Mostly she dresses that way to annoy her parents.'

'I'm guessing it works,' I said, giggling.

'Totally,' said Grace. 'But underneath, Suzie's really sweet. She adores animals, and helps out at the animal shelter every week.'

'But didn't she drop out of college?' asked Alice. 'Her parents can't have liked that.'

'She *did* drop out of college,' said Grace. 'But that was only because her parents made her do a computer course that she found totally boring. She's going to art college now, and doing really well. She won a big prize for sculpture a few months ago.'

'Did that make her parents proud?' I asked, kind of guessing the answer.

Grace shook her head. 'No. They didn't even go to the award night. They think art is a waste of time.'

'Oh,' I said, suddenly feeling sorry for the pale-faced girl who'd once scared me so much. I felt kind of stupid. Mum always gives out to me for judging people by the way they look. I know she's right, but usually I can't help it.

Just then the doorbell rang. Grace jumped up and looked out the window. When she turned back to us, she was smiling.

'OMG,' she said. 'This is going to be totally amazing.'

'What?' I asked. 'Is it a pizza delivery man — with a big stack of boxes with our names on them?'

'No,' said Grace. 'This is something much better. It's Witch-girl. She's all dressed up and it looks like she's got her hair done. I bet she's come crawling back for Gavin, and this time she's going to be totally disappointed. Come on, girls, you can't miss this.'

The three of us raced downstairs, and Grace opened the door.

'Hey, Kiddo,' said Witch-girl. 'Is Gavvy

home?'

She was pretty, but she had cold, hard eyes. She looked confident, and kind of mean, like if you got in her way, she'd trample right over you with her pointy-toed, high-heeled boots.

'I said, is Gavvy home.' she repeated. 'I haven't got all day.'

Grace was smiling at her in a way that must have been totally annoying.

Alice couldn't resist. 'He's definitely here somewhere, isn't he, Grace? But didn't you say he's Skyping his girlfriend?' she asked sweetly.

'*I'm* his girlfriend,' said Witch-girl, narrowing her cold eyes. 'Or I will be in a few minutes.'

'Hmmmm,' said Alice. 'I wouldn't be too sure about that.'

'He's in the living-room,' said Grace, pointing. 'Knock yourself out.'

Witch-girl went into the living room, and closed the door behind her.

'Leah,' we heard Gavin saying. 'What are *you*

doing here?' He didn't sound happy.

We couldn't make out the words, but we could hear Leah's voice, all sweet and syrupy. Gavin wasn't answering, and slowly Leah's voice became louder. It kept changing from begging to flirty to angry to whining like a spoiled toddler. It was totally weird, like there were five girls in the room with him, all fighting to be heard.

'But I told you I was sorry,' she kept saying. 'And you've always taken me back before. I don't understand what's changed this time.'

Gavin said something we couldn't quite catch, and then there was the sound of Leah's high heels marching towards the door. Grace, Alice and I raced upstairs, and sat on the landing.

We watched as the living room door opened, and Leah marched out. Her high-heeled boots click-clacked on the wooden floor. 'One day, Gavvy,' she said. 'You're going to wake up and realise that you've made the biggest mistake of your life – and then you'll be sorry.'

Gavin was standing in the doorway with his arms folded. 'I don't think that's going to happen,' he said calmly. 'I think I'll wake up and realise what a very lucky escape I've had.'

'Yessss!' whispered Alice. 'Go, Gavin. You tell her.'

Witch-girl tossed her silky hair, and stamped towards the front door. She stood with one hand on the doorknob and turned back and looked at Gavin.

'Because I'm a nice girl, I'm going to give you one last chance,' she said. 'But if I walk out this door, I'm not coming back. Ever.'

'Is that a promise?' asked Gavin.

Witch-girl hesitated for a second, and then she flung the door open, and went out, slamming it behind her.

Gavin went back into the living room, and Grace, Alice and I jumped up and down and hugged and laughed until our throats were sore.

Chapter Twenty-Four

Afew days later, I was lying on my bed with Domino curled up on my feet. I was in the middle of a really good book, when Mum came into my room.

'Sorry for disturbing you, darling,' she said. 'But I'm doing some baking, and I've run out of organic quinoa. Would you mind running down to the shop for me, please?'

I wanted to argue, but there was no point. Arguing with my mum is a total waste of time – she always has an answer for everything I say.

I got up from my bed and stroked Domino. 'Won't be long,' I said. 'Keep the bed warm for me.'

'Thanks, love,' said Mum as she handed me the money. 'And it's cold outside – be sure to wear your coat and scarf.'

'But Mum ......'

My mum can move like lightning when she wants to. Before I could finish the sentence, she'd opened my wardrobe, pulled out my jacket, and found the scarf that I'd hidden under a heap of old school-books. She wrapped the scarf round and round my neck like she was wrapping up a wriggly human present.

'There,' she said. 'Now put on your jacket and you'll be ready for anything.'

I loosened the scarf in an effort to breathe. It was the scarf Mum had knitted for my thirteenth birthday, and I have to admit, it was soft and warm. It was also brown and ugly. Worst of all, that scarf was like a Melissa-magnet. Every time I wore it, she showed up as if by magic, all ready to give me a hard time for having a mother who wants to save the world.

As soon as I had put on my jacket, Mum pushed me towards the door.

'Off you go,' she said. 'Organic quinoa, don't forget.'

★ ★ ★

I made it all the way to the shop and most of the way home without meeting anyone. I was starting to feel confident as I came up to the last corner before my road. Two more minutes and then I'd be safely back on my bed with my cat and my book.

And then I heard it.

'Hey, Megan, how's it going?'

I recognised the voice before I turned around. Melissa.

Why hadn't I run all the way home?

Why wasn't Alice with me?

Why was I wearing the ugly scarf?

'Hey, Melissa,' I said, as I continued to walk towards the safety of my home. 'I'd love to chat, but I've got to bring this stuff home for my mum. I've got to—'

But Melissa put her hand on my arm, stopping me.

'Before you go,' she said. 'There's something I ...'

Reluctantly I turned around to face her.

'That's the scarf your mum made for your birthday, isn't it?' she said. 'It looks totally—'

Suddenly I didn't want her to finish. It was like my brain was a pinball machine and all Melissa's old insults were rattling around inside it, making me feel sick and dizzy. I had to make her be quiet.

'Stop right there, Melissa,' I said. 'Don't say another word – not a single, solitary word. You've been picking on me and insulting me for years and years, and now I've had enough. I don't care what you think about me, or my mum or my clothes, or ... anything. I'm not going to let you bully me any more. It's over. Forever. Now, you should probably close your mouth, I think you might need a licence to catch flies around here.'

Melissa slowly closed her mouth and stared at me like she'd never seen me before. In a way, she hadn't ever seen me before. She'd only ever seen the scared Megan, the one who wasn't brave enough to stand up to her. I smiled to myself. I liked the all-new Megan.

'So anyway, Melissa,' I said. 'Sorry for interrupting you. What were you going to say about my scarf?'

'Actually,' she said. 'I was going to say that it looks totally soft and warm.'

Now it was my turn to be speechless. 'I'm not sure I believe you,' I said, when I finally found my tongue.

She gave a big sigh. 'It's the truth, but I don't blame you for not believing me. I know I've been kind of mean to you in the past.'

'*Kind of* mean?'

'OK,' she said with a small smile. 'I've been totally mean. I think I've worked out why, but

I'm not sure I can explain it properly.'

I was confused.

Was she playing some kind of mean trick on me?

Or was my timing all wrong?

Just when I was learning how to to cope with the old, mean Melissa, why had this new, nice one shown up?

What was going on?

I needed time to think. I put the organic quinoa down on the wall next to us, and folded my arms, trying to look like I was calm, like I was in control.

'So go ahead,' I said. 'Give it your best shot. See if you can explain why you've been picking on me ever since you've known me.'

Melissa took a deep breath. 'It's just that ... I think ... you see ... and I know this sounds kind of weird ... but ... I've always been kind of ... jealous ... of you.'

I was wiping the tears of laughter from my eyes, when I realised that she hadn't been joking. She was standing there, patting her shiny hair and looking as confused as I felt.

'I don't get why that's so funny,' she said.

'*You* jealous of *me*?' was all I could say.

'Yes,'

'But that's crazy. What exactly were you jealous of?'

'It started years and years ago, when we were little kids,' she said. 'When your mum used to wait outside the school for you every afternoon.'

I remembered those days. Mum used to stand right outside the school gate, and when I came out, she'd run towards me and hug me like she hadn't seen me for six months. Even though I was tiny, I used to be totally embarrassed.

'Your mum always looked so happy to see you,' she said. 'Like you were perfect. Like you were the centre of the universe. Mostly, I was picked up from school by a babysitter.'

'Yeah, but your mum had a job. She probably found it hard to get away in the middle of the day.'

Melissa shook her head sadly. 'Lots of the other mums had jobs, but still they found time to come to the school. Mine was the only one who never showed up.'

'But I remember your mum coming to pick you up one time,' I said. 'She had a briefcase and a laptop and she looked like someone important. I think that was the same day that *my* mum was in such a hurry, she'd forgotten to take her apron off. It was totally embarrassing.'

'Occasionally my mum did come,' admitted Melissa. 'When she had a day off from work. But when that happened she was usually late, and we had to run all the way home, so she could ready for some really important meeting. I always felt like I'd messed up her day, just by needing to be picked up.'

'Oh.' I couldn't think of anything else to say to that.

'And when you were little, your mum always had some special treat for you. I often heard her say, 'Look Megan. I've brought you a surprise.'

I rolled my eyes. 'Those treats were never a big deal. It was usually a bird's feather or a sugar-free cookie, or a chopped-up carrot or something pathetic like that.'

'Maybe,' said Melissa. 'But those treats were for you. Your mum had brought them especially for you.'

All of a sudden I remembered the heart-shaped stone my mum had given me one afternoon. It was still on the locker next to my bed. It's not exactly pretty or useful, but I like knowing that it's there. For the first time, I could see where Melissa was coming from.

She leaned across and touched my scarf. 'I remember the first day I saw this scarf,' she said.

'I remember that day too. I don't think I'll ever forget it. You mocked me and said it looked like a snake.'

'I'm sorry,' she said. 'I shouldn't have done that. It's just that ...... my birthday had been the day before. My mum was in London on business and it was very late that night when she called me. I think she'd forgotten until then that it even was my birthday. The next day, a courier showed up with a dress for me. It was really expensive and pretty, but it was completely the wrong size – I think Mum might have sent her assistant out to buy it or something. And then I heard Alice saying that your mum had knitted you a scarf, and I thought about how long that must have taken her.'

'Not that long really – she's a really fast knitter – and she doesn't get out much.'

'Whatever. She did it for you. She made you something special, and my mum …… well my mum would never, ever do something like that.'

'Oh,' I said again.

'And your mum is forever doing amazing things for you,' she said. 'Like the welcome home banner she made for you when you were in Lanzarote with Grace.'

'You saw that?'

Melissa smiled. '*Everyone* saw that. It was there for most of the week. I think your mum put it up half an hour after Lorna and Eddie picked you up to bring you to the airport.'

'That's totally embarrassing,' I said.

'Maybe it is a bit,' said Melissa. 'But mostly it's cute. It was really sweet of her to make that banner for you. It shows how much she loves you.'

'Your mum loves you too,' I said, hoping it was true.

'I know she does,' she said. 'It's just that she's not very good at showing it – and that's kind of a problem.'

I felt sorry for Melissa, but I still didn't understand what she was saying. How did all this explain why she felt it was OK to bully me?

'I'm sorry,' I said. 'But what's all this got to do with me?'

'I think I gave you a hard time – because I felt so bad. I know it's stupid but it was like, if I couldn't be happy, then I didn't want you to be happy either. Can you understand?'

I thought I could. Mum always says that

when someone does a mean thing, it says more about them than it says about you.

'And then there was Alice,' said Melissa.

'What about Alice? What's she got to do with this?'

'I've never had a friend like Alice. Every time I saw you two together, it made me feel bad about myself.'

'But in primary school you had lots of friends.'

She shook her head. 'They weren't real friends. Mostly they just hung out with me because they were afraid I'd thump them if they didn't.'

'But ...' I stopped when I remembered that Grace had said pretty much the same thing.

'You and Alice have this perfect best-friend thing going on,' she said. 'It's like, no matter what happens, she's got your back, and you've got hers. And I was totally jealous of that.'

I tried to imagine life without Alice, but I couldn't.

'And the other day, you and Alice and Grace did that really, really nice thing for me. Because of you, I won't be going back to boarding school in September. And it was so kind, and I'm so grateful, but I feel totally bad too, because I've always only ever done mean stuff to you.'

Maybe I should have argued, but how could I? Everything she said was true.

'I'm really, really sorry, Megan,' she said. 'Can you forgive me?'

I looked at her for a long time before answering.

She was the girl I'd hated for years.

She was the girl who'd made my life a misery.

She was pretty and cool, and her clothes were so nice, and thinking about her being jealous of me was just weird.

'Sure,' I said in the end. 'It's fine. Everything's just fine.'

Melissa gave a little squeal and then she leaned forward and hugged me. Her hair brushed against my face. It was totally soft, and it smelled like coconut and lemons.

OMG! I thought. *I'm hugging Melissa.*

And I couldn't quite make up my mind if it was a dream or a nightmare.

Chapter Twenty-Five

When Melissa finally let me go, I felt all weird and dizzy, like I'd been on a merry-go-round and had got off too quickly.

Melissa seemed fine though, like nothing strange had happened at all.

'I'll walk you home,' she said. I wasn't sure if that was a good idea, but I was so used to being afraid of her, I didn't argue.

'There's not much I'll miss about boarding school,' she said as we walked. 'The swimming pool looks good on the brochure, but it's never warm enough – and they put too much chlorine in it. The bedrooms are kind of small and dark. Most of the teachers are really cross. The only one I really like is the science teacher. She's big into the environment, and she's always telling us about how we should be saving the planet. She's really cool. Actually she … she reminds me a bit of your mum.'

I opened my mouth but no words came out.

Was Melissa actually saying that my mum was cool?

Was this the freakiest day of my whole life?

By now we were outside my house. We stood there for a second and it was a bit awkward. I wondered if I should invite Melissa in.

I tried to picture her sitting at the kitchen table, eating sugar-free cookies, and drinking pomegranate juice.

I tried to picture her having a discussion about global warming with my mum.

Some things are just too weird to imagine.

In the end, Melissa rescued me.

'I've got to go,' she said. 'Sorry again and thanks again. See you around.'

'Er….bye Melissa,' I said, but she was already halfway down the road, flicking her hair as she went.

★ ★ ★

Just as I opened my gate, Alice came running out of her house.

'OMG,' she said. 'Jamie is going to drive me totally crazy. One of his friends gave him a drum for his birthday, and he won't stop playing it. You've got to rescue me, Meg. You've got to take me for hot chocolate. I think that might be the only thing that will save my life. If I don't ...'

She stopped when she saw Melissa disappearing into the distance.

'Hey,' she said. 'Is that Melissa?'

I nodded.

'What's she doing around here?'

'We were having a chat.'

'Was she picking on you again? That's totally

mean, especially after all we did for her.'

'But—'.

'Maybe we should go around to her place and do a lot of crazy stuff and try to make her parents change their minds about sending her to our school.'

'She wasn't—'

'Maybe we should start a rumour that our school is going to close down because the teachers were caught stealing from the hockey-pitch fund. Or we could say that there's this weird virus leaking out of the science room. We could ...

She stopped talking when she noticed that I was laughing. Trust Alice to race off into crazy-plan mode, without stopping to find out if it was necessary.

'You only have to say the word, Meg,' she said. 'Say the word and I'll sort Melissa out for you. I'll get Grace and Louise and Kellie and—'

'Thanks, Al,' I said. 'But that won't be nec-essary. It's sorted. Everything's sorted. I'm not afraid of Melissa any more.'

'Megan!' she said as she hugged me. 'That's amazing. I'm so proud of you.'

'Now are we still going for that hot chocolate?' I asked. 'Or are you going to hug me to death?'

She let me go. 'Hot chocolate,' I think.

'Then give me one minute.'

Suddenly I realised that I didn't have the quinoa any more. I must have left it on the wall when I'd been talking to Melissa.

'OMG,' I said. 'Mum's going to kill me. Don't go anywhere. If the shopping's gone I'm going to need a bodyguard.'

I raced back to where I'd left the quinoa. Luckily it was still there. I guess organic quinoa isn't the kind of thing that gets stolen a lot.

I ran back home and went inside. I gave Mum the quinoa, stroked Domino, took off my scarf and hid it under the stairs.

When I went outside, Alice was still leaning on the gate.

'Ready?' she asked,

I nodded, and then I set off for town with my very best friend.

THE 'ALICE & MEGAN' SERIES
BY

<u>HAVE YOU READ THEM ALL?</u>

Don't miss all the great books about Alice & Megan:

Alice Next Door
Alice Again
Don't Ask Alice
Alice in the Middle
Bonjour Alice
Alice & Megan Forever
Alice to the Rescue
Alice & Megan's Cookbook

Available from all good bookshops

The 'Eva' Series
by

Judi Curtin

Don't miss Judi Curtin's great books about Eva and her friends

Have you read them all?

Eva's Journey

Eva's Holiday

Leave it to Eva

Eva and the Hidden Diary

Available from all good bookshops.